INFATUATION

SHIFTERS FOREVER AFTER

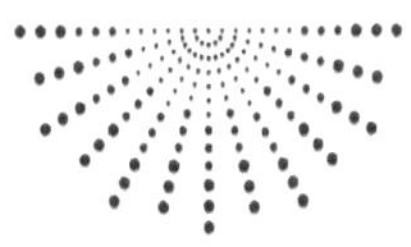

ELLE THORNE

Thank you for reading!

*To receive exclusive updates from Elle Thorne and to be the
first to get your hands on the next release,
please sign up for her newsletter.
Put this in your browser:
ellethorne.com*

INFATUATION

Moscow resident Hawke, Terrence Hawke, is a polar bear shifter on a mission. He's the witch hunter. His mission is to kill all witches in retaliation for the death of his sister at the hands of rogue witches. He and Vengeance are given a new assignment to capture a witch for trial with the Shifter Council. Sounds like it's right up his alley—being paid to capture and turn over an enemy, right?

Witch Alannah Autumn's sister left for Moscow to serve in an apprenticeship and now she's gone missing. Alannah packs her bags and with the help of Mikhail Romanoff, she's off to Moscow to find her little sister, Mireille.

What she doesn't count on finding is the sexy witch hunter polar bear shifter who has a spider as an accomplice and an aviary full of falcons.

Unravel mysteries, meet sexy new sorcerers, and find love with Alannah and Hawke.

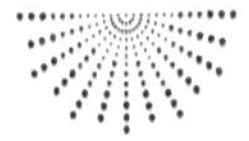

Witch hunter.

This was a moniker Hawke had earned. It was a nickname he reveled in, knowing every time he hunted a witch, he brought himself a little closer to feeling as though his little sister's death had been avenged.

Closure? There was no such thing. Not as long as a memory of his sister's broken and battered body lived in his mind. It was the same memory. It had made him a violent teenager, always in trouble with the Shifter Council. Though they had cut him slack, whispering he'd been through something that would have ruined a lesser man.

Who said it didn't ruin him?

That violent teenager he'd been made his way into the special forces of the shifter military, where he'd excelled at killing.

Witch hunter.

A wry, self-deprecating smile twitched the corner of his lip. He'd seen enough death, but didn't know a way to put aside the torment of his sister's death that haunted him.

He'd pay good money to learn how to give himself peace, but lately he'd begun to think the only peace he would ever have would come when he was six feet under.

This giant polar bear shifter of a man, a mountain, though not as bulky as some because he kept himself lean, was beginning to think he had fought the good fight and it was time to hang it up.

Maybe this will be the last job.

And maybe after this, he could go into a forever hibernation. He could leave the world and its pain and misery behind.

There she was.

The witch.

Coming out of her apartment in the outskirts of a small town near Moscow, Russia, not too far from where Hawke made his permanent home. She walked carefree as though life itself brought her special joy. Her lips curved into a smile, seemed like her soul shared a special secret with nature that granted her a charmed existence.

That smile of hers would be gone soon enough, once he turned her over to the one who hired him.

This witch would be taken to the Shifter Council to pay for her crimes.

Hawke had no use for witches. He never had, and never met a witch he liked.

Take that back, he had one use for witches. He glanced at Vengeance on his sleeve, a spider that cast enchanted webs which paralyzed and even poisoned witches. A witch had given him Vengeance in exchange for Hawke letting her live.

As if knowing he was thinking of her, Vengeance stirred, twitching one of her hairy legs, her eyes glancing in his direction. Vengeance was no small spider; she was larger than the palm of his hand. She'd been his friend, his best friend really, since about six months after Hawke left the special forces. He'd re-pledged himself to the task of seeking revenge, and Vengeance had taken to her name as if born to it.

The waiting was the hardest part. Hawke lay in hiding, patiently awaiting the return of the witch he was hunting. He had tracked her for days, learning her patterns, found out when the best time to take her would be and where.

She was a small thing, this witch, as far as height went, probably not even reaching him mid-chest. Though she was curvy, with dark brown hair that had auburn highlights and chocolate brown eyes.

Hawke knew better than to think for a split second that the height of a witch could determine the power within. He had faced a much shorter witch, and had the scars to prove it before he and Vengeance prevailed, banishing the woman to witch heaven.

Permanently.

Doubt there was a witch heaven?

All witches go to hell.

Of that, he felt certain.

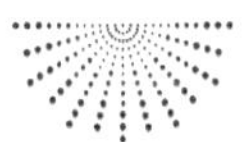

CHAPTER TWO

Alannah watched her cousin Fiona and Fiona's mate Jonah on the balcony of Mikhail and Miriam Romanoff's home.

They seemed so happy. Was it possible? Alannah had gone to one of the highest witches in a neighboring coven to ask for help for Fiona. She knew how important it was to Fiona that she be able to carry her shifter mate's baby full term. It was so rare that a witch could get pregnant with a shifter's baby, and actually carry it to birth.

Fiona had not indicated she was pregnant yet, nor had Jonah mentioned anything with his supersensitive shifter senses picking up the heartbeat of a baby or the scent of her pregnancy. But Alannah was on pins and needles. She felt responsible for their union, even though she wasn't sure that sense of responsibility wasn't misplaced. But still, she supported this union wholeheartedly, fear for the wellbeing of a baby aside.

She glanced down at her cell phone again. Seems that was all she was doing lately: waiting for Mireille to contact her.

Alannah's sister Mireille had gone to Russia to study her witchcraft arts.

You'd think she could find someone locally who would be able to teach her what she needed to know. But no, not Mireille.

Mireille had to learn from the very best. She'd heard through the grapevine there was a witch, a powerful sorceress, just outside Moscow. And just like that, Mireille packed her bags.

Alannah knew she had arrived there safely. She knew she was enjoying her stay there, except for the cold weather. Neither Alannah nor Mireille were wild about snow.

But now, three days had passed.

Actually, three days, four nights. And not a word from Mireille. No call. No text. No email. At first, her phone had rang and rang when Alannah called. Now it simply rolled straight to voicemail as if the battery were dead. Or the phone had been turned off. There was no way Mireille was turning her phone off, of this, Alannah was certain. Her sister would have known the amount of stress this would've caused Alannah. She would never have gone without communicating.

"Are you okay?" Miriam Romanoff, matriarch of the

Romanoff clan of polar bear shifters, though an Arctic fox shifter herself, wore an expression of concern.

Alannah glanced up from her phone. "I'm fine." She placed her palm over her phone and slid it into her lap, then rose from her seat. "Excuse me for a minute."

Alannah headed to her room in the Romanoff home. She was their guest, but it was beginning to look like she was their forever guest. She'd been staying with them since she helped Fiona and Jonah extricate themselves from the brouhaha they'd become emerged in with the Northfork witch coven.

Fiona, Jonah, and the Romanoff clan had emerged victorious, assisted by Alannah's intervention. But Alannah's integrity and honor in helping the Romanoff and her cousin Fiona, had put her in a bad place with Ilse, the leader of Northfork. She'd been banished from the coven. Though being away from Ilse was a bonus, Alannah did miss some of her friends at Northfork.

Realizing her homeless and coven-less predicament, the Romanoffs had been kind enough to take her in. Of course, Alannah's little sister Mireille had been invited, too, but Mireille who had not been living at Northfork, but rather staying an hour away, had passed on the offer.

Now Mireille was…

Alannah pushed that thought away.

Mireille is fine.

She was simply being irresponsible. She was being carefree, fun-loving, Mireille.

No she wasn't. She wouldn't do that to me.

Alannah closed the door to her room and pressed on her sister's photo on the phone screen. She waited for Mireille's phone to ring.

It didn't.

Mireille's cheery voice popped onto the cell phone immediately. "Hi. You've reached Mireille. You know what to do."

Alannah jabbed at the phone with her index finger, breaking the connection.

I know exactly what to do.

Exactly.

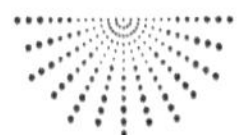

CHAPTER THREE

"Why are you keeping me prisoner?" the witch whispered.

Hawke wondered if she realized he could hear her. She was confined, a captive, thanks to Vengeance's enchanted web weaving.

He heaved an exasperated sigh, not buying her innocent act. "I have a decree from the Shifter Council. You're standing trial for executing shifters. They'll send a representative to pick you up and transport you there."

And it won't happen soon enough.

Her proclaimed innocence didn't hold water for Hawke. Neither did the fact that she looked innocent. He knew all about the deceptive ways of witches.

And come to think of it, he'd had enough.

He turned to Vengeance perched on a wooden rail

near his recliner. "I'm going to take a breather. Want to go or stay?"

She leapt from her perch, airborne for a brief second, then landed on his shoulder.

He moved toward the web the witch was enclosed in, a cage specially prepared for her by Vengeance and tossed food in. "Don't try to escape." He ran his fingers over the mesh of Vengeance's web. "It's escape proof."

She glared hate at him through her liquid brown eyes. He turned from her and pushed the thought that plagued him to the far recesses of his mind.

That witch is about the same age Renee would have been. If she were alive.

Renee. His sister.

Anger burned anew and he slipped upstairs in the dacha he'd bought a few years ago.

He'd been in Russia visiting his great-grandfather, the last relative on his mother's side still living in the country, when he'd run across the nineteenth century home. A dacha, his great-grandfather had explained, was a summer retreat home for Russians who were mid- to upper-class. He'd been unable to resist the architecture and had bought the abandoned building and several of the lots that surrounded it.

He locked the sturdy wooden door on the brick and wood structure, larger than a cottage, but not quite the size of some dachas that could double as a villa. He glanced back at the home. The basement where the witch was kept had blacked-out windows. It looked secure and wouldn't rouse suspicion. He'd sound-proofed the room as best he could and his property was fairly remote, so he could afford to step away for a spell to visit his aviary.

Hawke, Terrence Hawke, but commonly called Hawke, had a special touch with birds. Specifically, he had started as the unofficial go-to guy for peregrine falcons in the area. Then he'd become the expert on birds of prey. There was a reason for that. His mother was a falcon shifter.

A bit ironic, he thought, a falcon shifter mating with a polar bear that bore the last name Hawke. His mother went from being Belinda Vargas to being Belinda Hawke. And she delighted in telling him and Renee the irony of a falcon marrying a Hawke when they were younger. Hawke and Renee lost both parents when they were young, and then Hawke lost Renee.

Life had certainly changed for him.

He glanced at Vengeance perched on his shoulder. At least, he had her.

Pathetic, I know, calling a spider your best friend. A spider that casts enchanted webs. A spider you got from a witch who offered the spider to you so you wouldn't hurt her.

Shifters shouldn't get the jump on witches. They have the advantage of distance, if they are spell casters. Yet, I have my ways. Skills I've developed over a long time of fostering hate for that specific breed of supernaturals.

Bounties on witches paid well, and hers was a bounty he was more than willing to collect.

I wouldn't be lying if I said the world would be better off without witches.

Hawke pushed the thoughts away. He was going to a place of goodness. His peregrine falcons were waiting for him, all in various stages of rehabilitation, some with the hope to be released, some not.

He had a couple of locals who tended to them in case he was delayed in his efforts to hunt witches.

He pulled his ATV up to the aviary, and no sooner had he stopped, than Vengeance crawled out of the hood on his back. The spider preferred to ride on his back in the confines of the hood.

Probably staying safe from the creatures that would love to swoop down on her.

He was under no illusion that his birds of prey wouldn't love to make a meal of Vengeance. One almost had, once. Luckily, Vengeance scooted into the hood just as the falcon skimmed the tip of Hawke's head. Then again, what would have happened to the falcon if Vengeance had spun one of her webs. Those webs were as secure as steel, this Hawke knew for a fact.

Who knew? He hated to see either the falcon or the spider hurt. That happened long ago when Vengeance was still new to him. These days, Vengeance was an old hand at either looking out for the birds or staying out of their sight altogether.

He slipped on his gauntlet and entered the aviary,

larger than a football field, and was immediately greeted by Jester, his oldest and most faithful falcon.

Jester's shadow coursed over the snow-covered ground and at the same time, Hawke felt Vengeance scurry across his shoulder and under the hood on his back, settling in place.

Jester released a greeting, the sound piercing the quiet sanctuary, then he made a power dive toward Hawke drawing up short when Hawke raised an arm. The raptor studied Hawke with an intense dark eye, turning his head this way and that.

"Don't give me a guilt trip, Jester. I was busy. I know you've been well-cared for."

Jester shook himself as if to argue that point.

"Yeah, yeah, you're fine."

No sooner had Hawke finished that discussion, than Erethra flew around him in a tight circle, letting out shrieks to get Jester to give up the spot.

Jester knew better than to piss off Erethra. He spread his wings and made for the skies. Right after the pressure of Jester's talons released from Hawke's arm, Erethra took his spot.

"I hope you're not here to reprimand me, too," Hawke cautioned her.

She didn't move. Still as a statue, she studied him.

"Awww. Come on. Not the cold shoulder treatment."

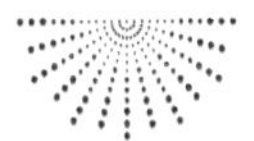

CHAPTER FOUR

Alannah shivered and pulled her jacket around her. *This is exactly why I don't like living in cold areas.* She could barely handle New York. She was thinking of moving.

Yeah, but not to this damned forsaken frozen land.

Come on, it's not that bad, she chastised herself. It really wasn't. And yet, she felt it was. Yeah. But that was because she couldn't find Mireille.

She'd flown in. Not exactly accurate. Mikhail Romanoff had arranged for her to fly in on his private plane.

Thank goodness for the Romanoffs, she thought, for what must have been the millionth time.

Mikhail had friends in Moscow who picked her up at the airport and delivered her to Mireille's apartment. With a whole lot of begging and quite a bit of bribing, Alannah had convinced the building manager to let her into her sister's apartment. Well, actually she'd also promised to have dinner with the old lecher, but she had no intention of following up on that part of the bargain.

Mireille's place had been left as if she'd planned to come right back. She'd had meat thawing on the counter, meat that now had maggots in it. Alannah shuddered at the memory of the wriggling white horrid little creatures.

She'd called Miriam as soon as she figured out that whatever had happened to her sister, it wasn't good.

"Hold on." Miriam's voice was muffled then she had handed the phone to Mikhail.

"The driver's on his way back. I just texted him from my phone. He'll take you to a wolf shifter that freelances. He'll track her. Call me when you find her. Don't put yourself in any dangerous situations. We can have boots on the ground there in no time at all to help you." He barked his orders, clearly a man accustomed to having his commands obeyed.

"Thank you, Mikhail."

"There's something else," he said.

She didn't like the tone of this voice.

"The witch's name you gave me, she's not in Moscow. Hasn't been teaching for ages. In fact, she's gone to the Hermitage."

The Hermitage, an isolated abandoned monastery tucked into the Pontic Mountains in Turkey. A place where witches went to disconnect from others, connect with their essential nature. It allowed witches to sharpen their skills.

"I'm going to send one of the boys there to Russia, just to be sure everything goes without any issues."

"I'm sure that's not necessary," Alannah countered.

"Maybe not. But I'll feel better if either Jonah or Isaac fly on over."

Alannah knew better than to argue with Mikhail. "Thank you."

They arrived at the address for the freelance tracker. The driver that Mikhail had arranged for Alannah was a few feet away at the end of the alley. She waited in front of a metal door, on a metal building, in an industrial area in Moscow. The only thought that came to mind was gray. Everything seemed gray, and it wasn't just because Mireille was missing. It was dreary and dingy.

And it made her feel hopeless about finding her sister. This wasn't the train of thought she wanted to have. She wanted to find her sister. Should she contact the police? Would they ask questions about why Mireille was here? If she told them she was here to study, would they want to know where? How could she tell her she was here to tutor under a witch?

So, here Alannah stood, looking for the tracker since she had no idea where to find her sister and no one she could turn to without arousing the wrong kind of suspicion.

She rubbed her hands together against the frosty weather and then knocked again.

Odd, how does knocking when your hands are cold hurt more than when they're not?

The door opened. An unshaven face peered at her from under an unkempt mop of blond hair mixed with steely gray. The eyes narrowed. "Da?"

"You speak English?"

More narrowing. The door closing slightly.

"Please. I need help. Do you speak English?"

"What do you want?"

"I'm looking for Anthony."

His jaw tightened, bristly hair moving with muscles that clenched and unclenched.

"I'll pay." She'd forgotten to use the magic words Mikhail had told her. He'd said nothing would get her as much help as money would.

The door opened a slight bit. "How much."

"A thousand dollars. Cash."

He practically drooled. "For what?"

"I'm looking for my sister. I heard you were a good tracker," she paused, suspicion at the forefront, "if you're Anthony."

"I am." He shook his head, making his hair fall back, allowing her a better view of a face that was lean and haggard with a hungry expression. "Let me get my coat."

He closed the door, not inviting her in.

Rude, she thought. But down deep, she was happy

about it. Judging from the smells that wafted from the room behind him, she wasn't sure she wanted to be in that stench.

She walked toward the car that had brought her here. The driver stepped out. All muscles and hardcore expression. "All okay?"

She nodded. "He's coming." *I hope.*

No sooner had she said that than the lean shifter in a denim jacket that had seen better days slammed the door to the warehouse behind him and strolled her way, a Cheshire cat grin barely concealed on his thin lips.

Until he saw the driver. He froze. "Who's he?"

"He's the driver."

"No. He looks like he's official. I don't do official."

The driver's face grew harder with a scowl. "What's the problem?" He addressed the question to Alannah, ignoring the wolf shifter.

Alannah shrugged, frustration setting in. This was not going to work. She had a sister to find.

She stormed and stomped her way toward the wolf shifter and grabbed his jacket by the lapels. She held her breath against the smell of it.

How the hell could a tracker—a shifter with supernaturally sensitive smelling abilities—stand that malodorous jacket. Or for that matter, his stinking home.

Still not breathing, she drew her face close to his, nose to nose. "Look. You're going to help me find my missing sister, and by damn, you're not going to give me a bunch of shit. Now I'll pay you—"

She gulped because she'd have to borrow more from Mikhail for this one. He'd already let her borrow some for the trip, but this would take away every penny. She wouldn't be able to buy a meal. Or anything. "—I'll pay you fifteen hundred dollars." She jerked on the jacket. "You got that?" She fought the urge to use magic on him. She knew shifters didn't usually care for witches, especially the uneducated shifters, and this one, he seemed like he hadn't made it passed third grade.

At first, she thought she scared the piss out of him, but then again, she wasn't that tall, or that formidable. So it wasn't likely she did.

But no, he was staring at something behind her. She chanced a peek.

The driver was standing directly behind her, his arms crossed over his chest. "The lady asked you a question."

Great. Let's hope he doesn't scare off the guy.

She gave the driver a sideways head nod, as if to say, get out of here, then said, "I got this. Thanks."

"He doesn't scare me," the wolf shifter grumbled.

Sure, that's why you almost pissed your pants. "He's not trying to scare you."

Well, actually he was, but damn it, Alannah needed results. She'd say Santa was real if the shifter would agree to track Mireille.

"You said fifteen hundred."

"I did."

"Show me. And half now, half after we find her."

"No." Mikhail had warned her not to give him a penny until he helped her find her sister.

Anthony did some grumbling under his breath, luckily she couldn't decipher it, then he said, "Fine."

"And don't ask to see it. Do I seem the nefarious type?"

She wished she hadn't asked that because he gave her the once over. She cringed at the feeling of his eyes checking her out, head to toe.

"Fine. Have your driver take us to the last place she was. Hopefully a place that has a heavy dose of her scent so I can track her." He looked at her feet. "You'll need better shoes than those. We'll be following her scent on foot. Surely, you don't think I can do it in a car." A sneer marred his already gaunt and creepy features.

As if I know how this scenting thing works. She bit her tongue and nodded. "I'll change at my sister's place. That's where we're going."

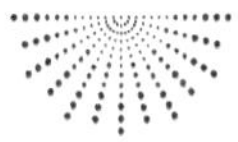

CHAPTER FIVE

This is ridiculous.

Alannah had been following the wolf shifter for hours. She'd sent the driver away, confident she'd be able to handle the wolf shifter herself.

I'm a witch, after all. I'm not some helpless, defenseless female.

Blisters dotted her feet, even though she'd changed shoes. They'd walked the entire day and now it was late afternoon and they were in the countryside. She was beginning to doubt he knew what he was doing.

"My sister wouldn't have a reason to come out here."

"I'm just following her scent. You want to get yourself another tracker?"

She blew out an exasperated breath and followed him.

"If it's any consolation," he gave her a sideways

glance, "the scent is stronger."

She perked up. "How much stronger?"

"She's been near here, and recently."

Suspicion clouded hope. He wouldn't just say that, would he? Should know soon enough if he wasn't lying, if they were close that was.

An hour later, just when she was giving up hope, they were on an empty country lane, one that led to nowhere it seemed. She took out her phone, ready to call the driver.

No signal.

No way!

Damn the luck.

"There!" The wolf shifter's voice was full of excitement. "I got her again. It's strong. She can't be far." He took off at a lope, heading through the trees.

Alannah's heart surged with a jolt, pocketed her phone, and took off after him.

Moments later, he drew up short. They were just exiting the wooded area. A home, old and isolated, faced them.

The wolf shifter raised his nose to the air and took a deep breath, his skinny chest expanding with the air intake. He pointed. "She's in there." Then an expression took over his face, replacing triumph with fear.

"My money." He held out a shaky hand. "Now."

"Not 'til I see my sister."

"Now." His voice shook.

"Our deal was that I find my sister. I don't see her."

"She's in there. Go."

"Go with me."

"You go. I'm not going any closer. I've met my obligation."

"I'm not paying you until I find her."

"I'll find you if you don't pay me."

And with those words from him, Alannah was stunned as his face lengthened. The excruciating sounds of bones stretching and tendons lengthening assaulted her ears.

Within a swift moment, he was transformed into a mangy, gaunt wolf with accusation in his eyes as he looked back at her then took off at a dead run, leaving Alannah there, alone, with a house that seemed empty.

All she had was his word that her sister was there. Something had scared him, but she had no idea what. It didn't matter, whatever was scaring the wolf shifter wouldn't keep her from finding Mireille if she was there.

Shivering against the cold, something she'd been able to push to the back of her mind in her urgency to find her sister, Alannah surveyed the house and made her way through the bush-dotted field lightly blanketed with snow. The snow crunched beneath her shoes that were adequate for a walk in the park, but had definitely not served her well on today's trek.

In front of the two-story, brick and wood home, the driveway was empty of vehicles, but it had tracks.

Tracks.

Someone came and went here. Someone lived here. Judging from the light covering of snow and the relatively small amount of snowfall, she'd say whoever drove that vehicle had left several hours ago.

Would they be returning? Was Mireille with them?

The hackles on Alannah's neck rose. She doubted this. If Mireille was fine, she'd have contacted her; she'd have responded to calls.

She approached the home, noting the darkness of all the windows, including the ones low to the ground that seemed to be in a basement. With a shrug, Alannah climbed the short staircase that led to the front door.

She rapped on the door lightly and then with more force.

No answer. No sound at all.

A few more knocks, insistent and loud, and still nothing.

She couldn't have said what prompted her to do what she did next. Something though, something deep within her said she needed to check this place out.

Now.

A sound within fueled her urge to go inside. Was it a thud or a voice? It was muffled, and it wasn't like witches were gifted with extraordinary hearing like shifters, so the sound was indiscernible.

Alannah sprinted from window to window, seeking an entrance.

Locked.

Locked.

Locked, also.

Tears of frustration threatened to flow and she was at the point of seeking a rock to break a window—

Not wise, she cautioned herself, *breaking into a house in a foreign country.*

But she didn't care. Something in her told her she needed to get inside.

Locked.

She ran to the next window on the back of the house, with one eye cast to the surrounding grounds, looking for whatever she was going to use to smash a window.

She was more than a little surprised when the window gave.

Unlocked.

She stood back in disbelief for a brief pause, then shoved it up enough to dive in, headfirst.

The place was semi-dark, the windows allowing barely enough light to see furnishings.

She was in one of the bedrooms, that much was clear.

Now what?

Now to canvass the house quickly, see if Mireille was here and get her the heck out of there.

And then I'll kick my little sister's butt for scaring the living daylights out of me by not returning calls.

One by one, room by room, she scoured the first floor, opening all doors, peeking into all closets.

Call it paranoia, but she didn't call out. She didn't

want to test her luck.

Nothing on the first floor. She'd cleared it in less than ten minutes.

On to the second.

Nothing on that floor either. Well, damn the luck. She also hadn't seen any of Mireille's belongings.

Could the wolf shifter have been that wrong?

Then a thought occurred to her.

Why didn't I think of that before? Or even first?

Now, she grew a bit apprehensive.

Scary shit happened in basements. In horror movies and real life. That's where people were held captive.

Don't be silly.

I'm not being silly, she argued with herself.

Okay, say no one was down there, still there were creepy crawlies.

And creepy crawlies scared the hell out of her. Alannah would rather deal with a rabid dog than an insect. Or a bat. Yeah, bats and rats qualified as creepy crawlies in her book.

Might as well get it over with. She sighed and went downstairs.

And as soon as I find nothing in the basement, I'll have to hoof it until I get to a place where I have a signal. Then I'll call that driver to come get me.

And after that?

After that, I'll call Mikhail and find out if he has a better tracker.

She found the basement door. Was surprised she'd

missed it, but then again, she had been thinking it was a pantry door. What else was she to think, it being in the kitchen?

She opened the door; it creaked.

Great. More horror flick effects.

She shuddered.

There was a light switch on the brick wall. Might as well, she certainly wasn't going to go poking around a basement in the dark, no sir, not a chance of that.

The light lit a naked bulb.

How much more unwelcoming could this be?

She found out when she took a step on the rickety staircase. More like a ladder, really.

One foot in front of the other, she made her way down the stairs.

The fourth one creaked.

Shit.

Relax, she cautioned herself. There's nothing down here to be afraid of. Nothing that will hurt me.

"Let me out of here!"

The screeching voice made her jump. She flinched and lost her footing, falling down the stairs, more than half a dozen of them and landed hard, face first, barely catching her fall with her palms.

Which burned like hell, now, from abrasions and scratches.

It took a few seconds for her to process that screeching voice.

Probably because she'd never heard her sister sound

like that. That had to be Mireille.

"Mireille?"

"Alannah?"

Alannah jumped to her feet, flinching because every part of her felt like it had been a punching bag after that fall.

The basement was segmented into separate cubby type rooms with thin partial walls that went up only five feet, not reaching the ceiling.

"Where are you?" Alannah ran toward the sound of her sister's voice, rounded one of the thin walls and stopped abruptly.

"What the hell…" she hissed at the sight before her.

"Don't touch—"

Too late. Alannah reached out and put her hand on the enclosure that held her sister captive.

She flinched and fell back from the jolt. "What is that?"

Mireille was in a cage that seemed to be made of silk threads. More like a cobweb, really, but thick, like a cocoon.

"What are you doing here?"

"You have to get me out before he returns. Hurry."

"How? I can't touch it."

"Grab that shovel." Mireille pointed to a corner. "See if you can pry the web loose."

"Web? Who put you here? What's this about?"

"Who?" said a very deep voice behind her.

Alannah whirled around.

CHAPTER SIX

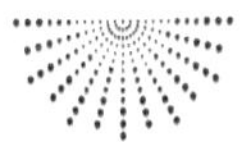

First things first, Hawke was definitely a man. So how could he not notice that delectable ass standing in front of his captive's cage.

Curved just right, tucked under, flaring at the hips, that was an ass unlike any he'd ever seen.

He swallowed and shook his bear. Damned bear. Between Hawke's bear and his testosterone…

You'd think I'd never seen a woman before.

Well, it had been a while, his bear responded.

The creature with that remarkable derriere was talking to his captive.

"Web? Who put you here? What's this about?" Sweetcheeks said to his prisoner.

Her voice. As delicious as that ass, even in the throes of panic, clearly.

Since when do I get excited about a woman's voice?

His bear roared in his head.

Simmer, he cautioned his bear.

"Who?" he said to Sweetcheeks.

She whirled around.

Holy hell, that face was better than that ass. Red hair twirled with her, full lips set in a thin line that did nothing to disguise their sexiness, emerald eyes shooting toxicity as if she'd kill him if he was a threat.

He couldn't resist the smile that came to his face.

"You." She stormed closer. Hands raising above her head. "You did this to my sister." She was fast. Her hands were high, and between them a blue flame flickered to life and grew.

Witch.

The same second he had that thought, Vengeance, who clearly had no love for witches, began to hiss on his shoulder. She raised on six legs, two legs thrust forward in her typical attack stance.

The emerald-eyed witch cast her hands down fast, flicking her wrists, sending that blue bolt of flame for his head.

Hawke dove for the ground as Vengeance leapt off his shoulder and set herself up a web line, dangling from the ceiling.

The witch squealed as, equally fast, Vengeance shot a line of her enchanted silk toward the witch's hands and bound them to her side.

The witch screamed in fury, unable to raise her arms, unable to cast that blue flame.

Who knows what other kind of spells she can cast.

"Put her in a cell, Ven."

Vengeance began her web weaving, swiftly putting the other witch in a cage not unlike the other.

In the background, the brown-haired witch was yelling at him from her cell. "Don't you dare hurt my sister!"

Figures. Sweetcheeks is a witch. And she's my damned prisoner's sister.

Great. Just great.

Would the bounty hunter that ordered the brown-haired witch want her sister? Were they both wanted by the Shifter Council?

Probably.

Ven was spinning away, the witch already enclosed in a cocoon, unable to move or break free. Then she'd remove the cocoon so the witch could move about freely within the confines of the cage.

"Why are you doing this?" More emerald daggers from those eyes.

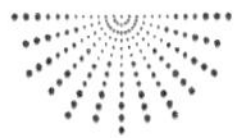

CHAPTER SEVEN

Alannah was confused. She couldn't move her hands, and she couldn't break free. And this man, this huge mountain of a man, was standing above her, watching, while his pet spider—she shuddered—was spinning a web.

"Why are you doing this?"

He didn't reply, just stood, eyeing that hairy legged, bug-eyed, beastie weave her into a prison.

That beastie was a magic spider of some sort. What else could it be? It was weaving a web around her she couldn't break free of. It had woven a web around Mireille that inflicted burns. For a man to have a magic spider, that meant he had to be a magic wielder.

"Are you a warlock? Some sort of sorcerer?"

He laughed at her. The nerve of him. He laughed at her question. Then his face turned hard. "Not a chance, Sweetcheeks."

"Don't call me that!" She wriggled to get free of the woven bindings.

The kind of spell she wanted to cast, she needed her hands.

Or maybe she could use a different spell. She closed her eyes, and when she opened them she released an enchantment, tossing a cage of her own his way. It was a red aura, traveling quickly, heading for the man.

The spider paused her weaving and hissed.

Alannah flinched.

Then the spider threw a web, intercepting Alannah's red aura cage.

"Blindfold her," the man ordered. "I didn't realize she was that strong a caster."

"Listen, you jerk."

"No, you listen, witch. You're in no position to—" He stepped nearer, getting close to her face. His dark blue eyes flashed a silver glow.

Oh my god. He's a shifter.

"What's a shifter doing with a witch's pet?" The words slipped out of her mouth before she could stop them or even rethink that idea of saying it out loud.

"Vengeance is no pet."

"Your pet spider has a name?" *And it was Vengeance?*

The spider paused its weaving around her and hissed a reply.

And it understands me. It's more than a pet. It must be a familiar. What else? But he's not a sorcerer.

Or was he part sorcerer, part shifter? That wasn't

impossible. It had happened before. Her cousin Fiona was a witch and a shifter.

"Keep talking, witch. I'll have Ven spin a gag for your pretty little mouth."

Like a threat would stop her. "Release me, and we'll see who'll do what to whom." She glared at him.

And then he walked out. Took the stairs two at a time and was gone.

While Alannah sat, processing what the hell had just happened, that damned hairy legged arachnid was spinning her a cage.

A cage. What for?

"How long have you been here?" she whispered to Mireille.

"Two days."

"He didn't—" Alannah couldn't bring herself to say it out loud. Though a part of her already knew the answer, somehow.

"No. He didn't. He hasn't laid a hand on me. He actually fed me."

A nice captor?

So this bothered Alannah even more in some ways because it reinforced an underlying feeling she didn't want to yield to.

"So, then, why?"

"He says he has a decree from the Shifter Council. That I'm to stand trial for executing shifters. They're sending a representative to pick me up."

"You?" Alannah fought the urge to laugh out loud.

"Doesn't he know you couldn't do that to save your life? That you're a healer?"

Mireille looked at Alannah through the thin webbing, then shrugged.

She was going to scream at him. And rail at him. And…

Alannah thought of the man.

He just doesn't look seedy.

There was a clarity in his eyes, a forthrightness, an honesty she couldn't remember seeing in too many men—especially not shifters.

Not that she didn't love shifters, she did. The Romanoff shifters. Most other shifters, she didn't really associate with.

Too many of them were like that damned wolf shifter tracker.

But this man, their captor, he had a look that screamed goodness.

And he was hot.

I didn't just think that. He's not hot.

Yes, he was. And he hadn't hurt her, even though she attacked him with her blue fire bolts. He couldn't be that bad, could he?

Then why is he holding us captive?

She refused to buy that crap about a Shifter Council.

Well, he hadn't hurt her sister. And he'd fed her. But what was this business about a trial?

"Hey!" She yelled for him, grabbing the silk bars Vengeance had created.

She jerked back, burned by the enchanted web. She looked at her hands. Scorched, red, almost to the point of blistering.

One glance at Vengeance confirmed the spider was watching her intently.

"You're a witch's pet. So why do you belong to a shifter, you big brute of a spider?"

Another hiss and the spider sped up the rate of her spinning.

CHAPTER EIGHT

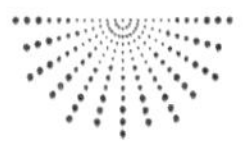

Hawke had to step out of the room and get things in order with his bear. With every breath that woman took, every word she spoke, his bear was going crazy in his head.

The pacing, the roaring, the growling, this was going to give him a headache of grand proportions.

"I'll be back, Ven." He turned his back on the spider and slipped up the stairs, taking them two at a time. He had no doubt Vengeance would handle the witch.

Just past the top of the stairs, he pulled out a chair and sat at the kitchen table.

What the hell was going on?

His bear, his testosterone, his dick. All of this was too damned much.

His bear paused, his rumbling softer, making snuffling sounds, no longer pacing like a rabid creature.

Hawke listened to his bear, heard his cause, tried to be impartial, finally he had to answer his bear.

No. She can't be. She's a witch, he told his bear. But Hawke knew it wasn't only his bear he had to convince; it was his own betraying body and mind also reacting to her.

Then it hit him.

Magic. She'd caused some sort of magic to make him feel attracted to her.

It didn't sound right, but what else could it be.

"Button it," he murmured to his protesting bear. "You're not always right."

Down below, the beautiful, green-eyed witch was bellowing. Who'd have thought she'd be able to get so loud. She could double as a drill sergeant.

He shook his head at his predicament. The brown-haired one wasn't an issue. This new one, the fire-brand, was. One deep exhale and he made for the basement door.

Less than a moment later, he was surveying the sullen, now silent witch. Then he walked past her. To his amusement, her jaw dropped. Seems she wasn't used to being ignored.

"What's her name?" he asked the brown-haired one, indicating the redhead with his thumb.

"Leave my sister alone," Sweetcheeks firebrand snapped.

He gave her a quick glance, then turned to

Vengeance perched on the nearest shelf, watching them.

"If that witch opens her mouth again, weave her a gag."

"Oomph." The witch clamped her lips shut.

Turning back to the brown-haired girl, he noted her frightened, wide eyes. "Well? Your name?"

Her eyes rolled up, only white was showing. No sooner did that happen, she collapsed, then began to convulse.

She flopped around in the cage, her body jerking against the webbing Ven had woven. With each contact her body made, a sizzling sound ensued. Right after that, she'd jerk away from the point of contact, but did it so violently, she bounced herself right back onto the voltage.

"Fuck." The little witch was burning herself on the cage.

He didn't hear his own expletive, and it took a second to realize why.

Behind him, the firebrand was screaming bloody murder. Yelling at him to help her sister.

He whirled on her. "What the hell is going on with her?"

"She does this. She has these episodes. Help her, please! Get her out of there. She's—"

The brown-haired witch was burning. The air was thick with the smell of her scorched skin. It would have been bad for a human's nose, but for a shifter's sensitive smelling senses, it was overwhelming.

Hawke allowed his bear to release claws on one of his hands and he shred the fabric quickly. Luckily, Ven's webs neither contained nor harmed him.

Within seconds, he had an opening wide enough to step through. He entered the cage and picked up the thrashing witch.

Hell, I hope she's not faking and doesn't suddenly cast a spell on me.

The other witch had finally stopped her infernal screaming, thankfully, because he'd been ready to tell Vengeance to shut her up with a carefully placed weave.

Holding the brown-haired witch against his chest, he carried her out. She was still thrashing, but it had lessened. She was angling in toward him as if seeking protection.

"What's wrong with this witch," he asked Firebrand as he sat on a trunk.

"Her name is Mireille, you d-bag."

He looked at her like she'd gone crazy. She had more guts than anyone he'd ever met, male or female. He brushed hair away from Mireille's face and winced at the sight of the burns she had on her cheeks and forehead. He glanced at her exposed arms. There too. Angry red slashes with blisters.

"What's wrong with Mireille?" he asked her sister.

Firebrand's shoulders slumped as if in defeat. "She's done this since she was a kid. Some sort of seizures."

"Why hasn't she seen a doctor?" Not that he'd call one to come here. Not now. Not with them being held as captives in his home. *Yeah, that wouldn't do.*

The firebrand sighed. "It's a witch thing. A human doctor wouldn't do."

"So then why haven't the witches taken care of it?" Right after voicing that, he asked himself why he bothered. Did he even care about witches anyway? The answer was clearly no, but yet, here he was with one in his arms, holding her like a little child, protecting her from whatever it was tormenting her body and mind.

"It's complicated." Firebrand set her jaw, as if not willing to answer anymore.

Mireille was still having tremors, though, at least she'd stopped thrashing.

"Please, let me hold my sister. I swear, I promise, on everything I hold dear, I will not do anything. Please."

He didn't want to. But he had one image that kept returning to his mind.

Renee's broken body and how he never got a chance to hold her. The shifters there to clean up wouldn't even let him get close enough to hug her. Said there was too much devastation.

"Ven." He nodded to the spider, who'd been watching them carefully from the shelf. "Let her out."

"Thank you," Firebrand managed between tears

streaming from her eyes. Tears that the little spitfire was clearly trying to hide.

"If she tries anything, Ven. Put her back in a cage. And then gag her."

He was still the witch hunter, after all.

Vengeance leapt from her spot on the shelf. Using a line she'd made herself, she swung across like it was a vine in a jungle. She alit on the cage, and with precision, sliced through her own woven web, allowing an opening large enough that the witch stepped through.

The witch came closer, sat next to him on the trunk, put her hand on her sister's forehead.

"What's your name, witch?" He couldn't keep thinking of her as Firebrand or calling her Sweetcheeks.

As if caught off-guard, or not realizing who she was talking to, or maybe she was involved in checking on her sister, she murmured, "Alannah."

Alannah.

The way she said it, it was like hearing a sigh on an ethereal wind. It flowed through him. Touching him in places he didn't think he had anymore, striking chords and emotions that he'd have denied existed if ever asked.

He let the name roll around in his mind. His bear roared. Hawke tuned out the bear. This was the time for logic, not to be driven by emotion or nature.

Mireille was beginning to settle, but that made her burns even more obvious. Guilt plagued him.

Why? Why do I feel guilty that she's burned? She's wanted by the Shifter Council to stand trial for killing shifters.

But yet, she looked and seemed so innocent.

It'd be a lot easier to believe the Firebr—Alannah, he corrected himself—had been the killer of shifters.

Though there was a part of him that denied this. She simply did not seem like one to do that.

"I have salve that will help her with the burns. How long is she usually unconscious when this happens?"

"Thank you. Please. It varies."

"I'll get it." He moved Mireille into her sister's arms. "Ven will be watching you." He voiced the warning, though he didn't feel he had to. He didn't think she'd try anything.

"As if I can carry my sister out of here."

True. But he didn't want to agree with her. Plus, her sister could wake, and then they could try something. Though he didn't think Mireille would be in a condition to do anything, even after she did wake. Those burns were going to hurt like hell.

The salve would help. He made for the stairs and again took them two at a time, trying not to be too loud, not wanting to disturb Mireille.

He found what he was looking for in the back of the cabinet above the sink. He'd not used it in so long that the seal was stuck. It had been left over from the time he'd spent in the military. He pushed the thought away.

Days he'd rather not think of. Days when he'd tried to deal with losing Renee.

Back in the basement, he held the jar out to Alannah. "This will do the trick."

"Are you sure?"

"Trust me," he said softly.

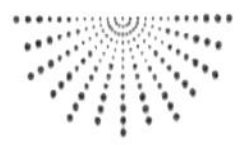

CHAPTER NINE

Trust him? How can I trust him when I don't even know him? Alannah dipped her finger into the jar and found herself touching something the consistency of petroleum jelly, but with a cool temperature and a light tan hue.

She raised it to her nose and sniffed, her eyes on the large man. It didn't have an odor. And it didn't seem to be affecting her fingers. She dabbed a bit on the top of her hand.

No effect.

Maybe she could trust him.

"I don't even know your name." She bit down on her lip. She hadn't meant to say that.

He frowned, not in anger, but almost in confusion. "I'm Hawke." His voice was a deep baritone, deeper than it had been before.

She studied the face that belonged to this man

named Hawke, looking for signs of deception, but instead, she found honesty.

How can that be?

He had a strong jawline, deep set eyes that glowed with an intensity that shook her to the core. Lips that were full, but not unmanly.

Who was this man who'd abducted her sister and held her for the Shifter Council? Mikhail Romanoff had connections with the council. Alannah needed to ask him for yet another favor.

She rubbed the salve over the burned areas on her sister's face. The urge to hurt him, to use her magic to destroy him and his spider was great. Maybe not as great as it had been earlier, for he was helping them, after all.

"And after this? Back to our cells?" She chanced a glance away from her task to ask him the question.

He didn't answer. His eyes were glued to her face, it almost made her uncomfortable.

And it did something else to her.

Something she didn't want to define and surely didn't want to admit.

What the heck kind of name was Hawke, she wanted to add.

"Why are you holding us?" she whispered.

CHAPTER TEN

Hawke found himself in the odd position of not knowing how to answer that.

He studied her face, unable to tear his gaze away. Her nose was tipped just so, as if it were as stubborn as she. Her hair caught the scant sunlight from one pinprick of a hole in the blackout curtains. It gleamed, bringing to mind a burnished antique metal. Her eyes, that green, almost unreal they were so green. Her face, shaped like a heart on a body that just didn't quit.

This woman was dangerous, and a risk to his cause. He steeled himself against her charms. Charms she clearly didn't know had an effect on him.

She'd finished applying the lotion. He capped the jar and set it next to her. "For later, in case she needs it."

Mireille looked like an innocent kid. He couldn't get past that. He wondered then, if there was a chance that perhaps the sister that they sought was Alannah.

"I'll show you," he told her. He'd verify his reasons with this.

He checked to be sure Ven was still on guard duty. The spider's eyes were moving left to right, ever vigilant, then he headed toward the filing cabinet in the corner.

Hawke pulled a file out and flipped through papers.

The name on the sheet was clearly Mireille Autumn.

"Here." He held it out to her. "See for yourself. Shifter Council. Your sister's name. A summons to appear. Here's my contract." He handed her the final page.

Alannah took them from him, laying them across Mireille's arm, who was still in her lap. Surely her legs were going to be numb shortly from holding her little sister.

She scanned the first page, then the second, the last, then went back to the first.

He took this opportunity to study her features, noting an errant series of freckles on the bridge of her nose that he wanted to touch, first with a fingertip, then with his lips.

Her profile was patrician, at the same time, hinting at a wildness deep within.

She spent a long moment on the first page again, before finally announcing, "I don't think this is real."

"How can it not be real? Who would do that? To what end?"

"How do I know you didn't manufacture this?" she snapped.

"How do I know they didn't pick the wrong sister. Mireille doesn't seem like the type to harm a fly. You, on the other hand."

"What?" Her voice started out strong then transformed to a hiss as she looked down at Mireille out like a light. "I can prove it. With a phone call to Mikhail Romanoff. If you even know who that is."

"I served with a Romanoff in the Middle East. Malachi Romano—"

A creak on the stairs caught his attention. He snapped his head in that direction.

Alannah did the same.

A voice came from the dimness around the corner. "Isn't this cozy?"

It was the one who'd given him the papers, who'd offered the bounty for Mireille Autumn.

Alannah gasped. "You. I should have put this together." Then she looked at Hawke with pure disgust in her eyes. "You're in on this."

He glanced from the one that hired him to Alannah, then back. How did they know one another? What the hell did Alannah mean?

He rose to his feet, stepped away from the trunk, and cast a glance at Vengeance to make sure she was at attention because he had a feeling shit might just get real.

CHAPTER ELEVEN

I lse.

What the hell was Ilse doing here?

It hit Alannah like a ton of bricks. Ilse and this shifter called Hawke were in collusion. But why?

She recoiled at the sight of the Krauss coven leader who'd been the head chair of Northfork the last time Alannah had seen her. Northfork, the guild of witches in northern New York state, touching on and actually in part of Mikhail Romanoff's territory.

Alannah heard there'd been an upset of the leadership at Northfork after she'd helped the Romanoffs save Fiona from Ilse's nefarious plans. Fiona, a witch and falcon shifter hybrid, was in imminent danger under Ilse's thumb.

Until Alannah and the Romanoffs stepped in.

And now, Ilse was here.

Probably for payback.

With him.

"You disgust me," she said to the shifter. She ignored the confused look on his face. He was clearly more than adept at acting. So sure, why wouldn't he pretend to be surprised? She glanced at the still unconscious Mireille. She'd move slightly and let her lay on the trunk while she took care of the betraying duo. "And you, Ilse, you've brought anything that's happened to you on yourself."

The spider was perched on the shelf, her front legs raised, hissing up a storm.

Well, hell, I'll just have to take care of all three. The spider, the shifter, and the witch.

Hawke rose to his feet, stood between Ilse and Alannah.

What the hell is he doing?

As if matters couldn't get worse, that was the precise moment Mireille awoke, mumbling and moving about.

Alannah swiftly disengaged herself and left Mireille on the trunk, stepping to the side so if Ilse did cast a spell, Mireille wouldn't be hurt as collateral damage.

"I should have known. The two of you are working together." She glared at Hawke.

Hawke moved to the left. "I don't know what you're talking about. I freelance. I showed you the papers."

"And I told you they're fake. I can prove it. With one phone call."

Ilse watched them, an evil gleam in her eye. "Tsk. Tsk. Tsk. How adorable. A lover's spat."

Hawke whirled on Ilse. "Why is she saying the paperwork is fake, witch?"

Alannah watched the exchange with interest. Was it possible he didn't know?

Surely not. No one would have abducted Mireille without knowing about Ilse. Would they?

"I'll deal with you later, shifter," Ilse snapped, then turned to Alannah. "You cost me my position. I was removed as chair at Northfork. They've appointed an interim until they find a replacement for me. Then my coven decided I clearly wasn't able to handle matters, so they took that from me. Then they expelled me. It's time for you to pay. I'll have my redemption and I will get my place back."

Ilse raised her arms, hands to the sky. Between her palms a red and green orb pulsated.

Vengeance hissed and spat a silk line at Ilse.

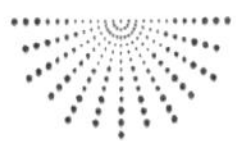

Hawke wasn't pretending to be confused. He had no clue what sort of undercurrents were going on between these two witches, but he had a feeling the gaunt witch in black had misled him. Maybe Alannah had told him the truth. Maybe the documents were fake.

"What's going on?" Mireille's voice had that out-of-it quality as she blinked and rubbed her eyes.

He felt like he'd stepped into the middle of a gunfight, unarmed, as far as information went.

Then again, it wasn't like he had much time to consider the matter.

Ilse was preparing to cast what looked like a green and red fireball.

Ven shot a line at Ilse and it caught the ball of fire as it made its way toward Alannah. The orb, surrounded by Ven's enchanted silk, fizzled and fell to the basement's concrete floor.

Hawke was stunned. Vengeance had come to him from this very witch. He'd have thought the spider would have been true to Ilse. And yet, Ven chose Alannah over Ilse.

"You." Ilse turned on the spider. "You're not supposed to attack witches. You pathetic, miserable little creature."

Alannah flung her hand toward Ilse, sending a shower of blue darts in Ilse's direction.

Ilse performed a swift pirouette, her black dress swirling about. A white aura surrounded Ilse, rendering Alannah's darts useless as they deflected from the shield and scattered.

Mireille cried out as one of the enchanted darts caught her in the shoulder.

Hawke slapped a hand on his chest where blood was flowing, one of Alannah's darts embedded in his flesh.

Ven hissed.

Ilse flicked her wrist, sending a red cascade of energy hurtling toward Ven.

Hawke roared and lunged, intercepting Ilse's spell.

"You can no more protect that spider than you could your own mewling sister, shifter."

Except he did protect her and then he fell to the ground, motionless.

Alannah didn't have the time to figure out what Ilse

meant. She needed to act. She gathered her energies preparing to attack again.

Ilse flipped her wrist, this time toward Alannah.

But the spider was faster.

Ven cast another web toward Ilse, this time, the witch wasn't quick enough to avoid the spider's web flinging. Ilse was wrapped in the line, hands bound as Alannah's had been. The webbing surrounded her legs, forcing her to the ground.

Alannah glanced from the fallen Hawke to her bleeding sister, and ran to Mireille, tears blinding her eyes, almost making her trip over her own feet.

I will never forgive myself if my own weapon killed my sister.

Alannah had accidentally almost killed Mireille when they were kids and horsing around. That's when they learned that Mireille was highly affected by Alannah's magic.

Ven spun her web with supernatural speed and before Alannah could react, Ilse was in the beginnings of an enchanted cocoon cage.

Alannah took Mireille's head in her arms, softly whispering a prayer, though she was not sure whom she was praying to. Please don't let my sister die; please don't let my sister die. She stroked Mireille's head, pushing the hair away from her forehead.

Mireille gasped.

Thank goodness. She's alive.

Mireille's eyes fluttered. "Is it over?"

"It's over."

"What about Hawke?"

"He's hurt."

Mireille raised her head. "How bad?"

"He's not moving." She looked at the man who'd fallen. She prayed he was still alive.

Vengeance was scurrying toward Hawke, making leaps across the floor. She crawled onto his chest, then went close to his face. Then, Vengeance did the strangest thing. She looked at Alannah.

"I think she's trying to communicate with you," Mireille said.

"She's a spider. That's not likely."

"How do you know she's not the victim of a transformation spell?"

Alannah look at her sister. "I don't." She shook her head. "But I do know she was your warden. And mine."

"She's on our side now."

From the cocoon, Ilse said, "You two are pathetic. I can't believe this. Are you witches? Or what?"

"Not your brand of witch," Alannah said. "Vengeance, please gag her. Stifle that witch before I kill her."

Vengeance wasted no time shooting out a line of silk that immediately put an end to Ilse's speaking.

"Killing her doesn't seem like a bad idea, right now." Mireille sat up. "Check on Hawke."

Alannah had already noticed his chest was moving. The large shifter was breathing. But she also noticed a lot of blood streaming out of his body. "We need to get him some help. I don't think I can stop the bleeding on my own."

"I haven't learned how to heal shifters yet. So what are we gonna do?"

"If I had a signal, I could call Mikhail."

"This is his home," Mireille pointed at Hawke. "I'm sure his phone works."

That was the best idea she'd heard thus far. Alannah jumped up, approached Hawke, then dropped to her knee beside him.

She kept one eye on Vengeance. Let's face it, she still wasn't fond of spiders, even if this one had been on her side during a fight against Ilse.

"Easy, Ven." She borrowed the nickname she'd heard Hawke using. "I just want to get his phone so I can get him some help, okay?"

Yeah, okay, I may just be certifiable. I'm asking a spider for permission to touch a shifter. And I'm acting like she knows what I'm saying.

Well, doesn't she? She did gag Ilse when Alannah had asked her to, after all.

Alannah gave the spider another look. *Just what are you, exactly? You're more than a magic spider, aren't you?*

She wasn't about to voice that bit of madness out loud. No sir, no how.

Alannah kept her eyes pinned to Hawke's face while she dug in his front pocket. If he woke and found her doing this—she blushed. Then she chastised herself.

Of course, he's not going to think I'm making a pass at him. He's going to think I'm trying to kill him.

Okay, that was good enough reason to work faster. Much, much faster.

Eureka!

She took the phone out and hustled back to Mireille's side, releasing a shudder at being so close to the arachnid.

"Still not wild about spiders?" Mireille teased.

"Lower your voice," she hissed at her sister. "That thing does understand English."

Mireille giggled.

She gave her a dirty look. "He's breathing, by the way. So that's good. And his color's good."

"He's hot."

"Mireille! He kidnapped you. Stop that."

Mireille gave her a sly smile. "Sure thing, sis."

"He is. He could die, and he was saving us."

"Actually, he was helping us, but he was saving his spider. If he dies, it's because he gave his life for her."

Alannah glanced at the eight-legged creature still on Hawke's chest.

Vengeance cocked her head, just a slight tilt as though listening in.

"Could you stop talking about her like she's not here?" Alannah whispered, a bit nervous. That spider could take them both out if she had it in her mind. Or she could inflict a whole lot of damage, if not.

She fumbled with the phone. "Not locked." That

could have been ugly if it had been. She dialed Mikhail Romanoff's cell phone.

"Romanoff." His voice was brusque.

"It's Alannah. I'm on a borrowed phone. There's this shifter here. He's bleeding. Unconscious, and I don't know how to treat or help him. I know your kind goes into hibernation to heal. How do I even get him to do that?"

"Slow down." On the other side of the line, Mikhail was saying something.

She heard Miriam's voice in the background.

"Miriam's calling Jonah on his cell. He and Fiona are in Russia. They're with the wolf shifter tracker. They've hired him to take them to the last place he took you."

"I'm exactly where that wolf shifter left me. In the house across the field at the end of the drive."

Relief flooded through her. She put her hand over the phone and whispered to Mireille, "Jonah and Fiona are close. Miriam's calling them on her phone to find out where."

Mikhail came back to the call. "Miriam told them. He said they're not far. Who's the injured shifter?"

"He said his name is Hawke. That he knows Malachi from the Middle East. He…" Of all the damned times for tears to start coming to her eyes. This was ridiculous. Unbelievable. She coughed and cleared her throat. *Am I really getting emotional about some guy I just met?* "He saved us." She could have added he was the reason they were imprisoned in the first place, but at this point, it seemed he thought he was serving the Shifter Council.

"What happened?"

There was a loud knock above her head.

"Oh. I think they're here. Let me call you back, Mikhail. My cell doesn't have reception, so I think this number's the best way to reach me."

"Keep me posted."

Alannah handed the phone to Mireille. "I'll get them." She glanced at Hawke. "Keep an eye on him."

CHAPTER THIRTEEN

Hawke had an awareness. He was wounded, sure, but his bear was keeping him from dying. His bear was trying to heal him at a faster rate than he was losing blood, but Hawke knew it was a losing battle, long term.

He was hoping his bear would put him into a hibernation so he wouldn't die. But the bear refused to do so. He refused to on two counts. First, he didn't want to abandon Alannah, and second, he didn't feel a hibernation would be safe, because he'd be vulnerable the whole time he was out.

Oh, and I'm not vulnerable, right now? While I'm lying on this cold ass concrete floor bleeding out?

Anger served no one for the bear had ignored his arguments.

At least, give me my body back so I can get up and do something, for Pete's sake.

No luck, again. The bear had totally shut him out.

You'll pay.

That was all Hawke had, an empty promise for retribution.

And he was sure his bear knew he didn't mean it.

He felt Vengeance on his chest, not much to her, almost feather light. She was standing guard over him as he figured she would.

His bond with Vengeance had been strong from the get go.

And that's why you'd risk our lives? For a spider?

Oh, now his bear was back?

It was Hawke's turn to do the ignoring. He refused to acknowledge his bear's question.

It wasn't that Hawke didn't understand his bear's feelings for Alannah. Hell, Hawke felt strongly about her too, it was just too…

Confusing.

In the back of his mind, he could hear Ilse's muffled protests. Clearly, Vengeance had applied a gag on the witch.

There was something that witch said he wanted to know more about. Something about his sister. What the hell had she said? He couldn't remember now, maybe because it was the heat of the battle. Or maybe because she shot him with that bolt.

What had she said about Renee? Something about her mewling.

Damn it all to hell.

He couldn't remember, and for some damned reason, it meant so much to him.

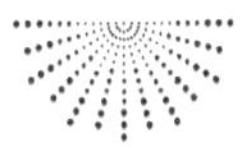

CHAPTER FOURTEEN

Alannah didn't even bother looking to see who was at the door. That's how eager she was to get Hawke help. She threw the door open.

And promptly fell back.

Ilse's second-in-command from Northfork. As tall and lean as Ilse, her gaunt face was tightlipped and her eyes widened in shock.

"You."

"Me." Alannah raised her hand to cast.

The second—why couldn't she remember her name?—snapped her hand up, quicker and more lethal than Alannah remembered.

Her hand erupted into a hook that latched around the back of Alannah's neck and jerked her forward, out of the house, onto the porch, then tumbling down the stairs and landing on the snow-dusted ground. Hard.

"Where's Ilse?" Second said.

The hook the witch had turned her hand into became a steel wire noose, tightening around Alannah's neck. She gasped, eyes watering from lack of oxygen. She couldn't answer if she wanted to; she was crushing her larynx.

Have… to… cast… before…

Too late. The hope she'd have enough strength to spell before passing out was gone. Pinpricks of light dotted behind her eyelids as they lowered.

In the distance, she heard a falcon shrieking. The shriek was louder, then louder, finally it was followed by a scream.

The noose loosened.

Alannah gasped for air. Everything was darkness and flashing white dots. She tried to gain focus while using her other senses to ascertain what was happening, but she couldn't tell. All she could hear was a tussle.

Calling as much mana energy as she could, she cast a spell of protection around herself, knowing it wasn't perfect but might protect her from some of the spells cast against her, depending on the spell caster's skills.

She rubbed her eyes, finally finding things coming into focus.

A large falcon was perched on a nearby branch while the Second lay at the foot of the tree, bloody and broken.

I know that falcon.

"Fiona?" Could that be her cousin Fiona? Why would she be in her falcon form?

She shook her head to clear her vision, but before she could fully focus, the falcon shrieked and flew away.

Alannah rose to her feet. She'd get the phone and call Mikhail, find out where Fiona and Jonah were before anymore of Ilse's allies could come forth for another attack.

Alannah was too weak to survive the next bout. With a final glance at Second's body, verifying from a distance that it was unmoving, Alannah made her way up the stairs, holding the banister to keep from falling. On the last step, she paused and leaned against the column to catch her breath. Her throat felt on fire on the inside and rubbed raw on the outside. She didn't even want to touch the tender, tortured skin on her neck for fear of hurting more.

The sound of a car's engine approaching caused her to turn and look at the driveway. The vehicle, a large, government-type SUV pulled up and hit the brakes. Out jumped Fiona from the passenger seat and the wolf shifter tracker from the backseat. Jonah exited the driver's side.

Fiona ran up the porch. "Are you okay?" She took Alannah in her arms and stared at her neck. Then she glanced at Second. "What the hell is she doing here?"

Alannah opened her mouth to tell her cousin it was a long story, but all that came out was a dry croak.

"Don't worry. I'll take care of this." Jonah took two leaps and was at the top of the stairs and heading for the front door.

"I've done my part," wolf shifter Anthony said.

Alannah thought he should have been a chicken shifter, not a wolf shifter.

He gives wolves a bad name.

And with that, the wolf shifter had turned on his heel and started through the field, taking the same path he'd brought Alannah down.

"He wouldn't have been much help anyway."

Alannah swallowed hard. "Were you here earlier?" She looked at the fallen body of Second.

"What?"

"Did you do that?" She pointed to dead woman.

Fiona studied her hard. "Witches are not to kill other witches. You know this."

Alannah nodded, unsure if she'd been answered or not. If Fiona, didn't do it, then there... She pushed the thought aside. She didn't want to think on it. She wanted full deniability if anyone ever asked if Fiona had killed Second. "I need to check on Mireille and Hawke."

Fiona gave her an arm to hold to steady herself as she helped her into Hawke's home.

Downstairs in the basement, they found an angry Jonah glaring at Ilse. Mireille looked petrified, sitting on the trunk. When she saw Alannah, she jumped up and ran into her arms.

"I thought Jonah was going to kill Ilse, if he could have gotten into that cocoon cage."

Fiona studied the scene before them and crossed her arms over her chest.

"Ilse. How fortuitous to run into you again." Sarcasm laced her words. "So it would seem you've tried to set up my cousin. Eager to have her pay for your misguided attempts to destroy Northfork by leading them down the wrong paths?"

Alannah gasped. "How did you know?"

"It wasn't hard to put together. Not to mention, her people—I mean flunkies—are as fickle as any traitor would be."

Jonah was leaning close to Hawke, his head next to Hawke's.

Alannah wondered what he was doing. Was he talking to Hawke?

"I need some privacy with him. Can you take this upstairs? He'll need to hibernate heal and I don't see that happening with all this fuss."

"What about her?" Alannah pointed to the wildly gesturing Ilse waving her arms about and making muffled sounds that didn't pass as speech.

"Take her out of here. Fiona and you can surely cast something that will overpower her."

"We can't break through that cocoon. It will burn." Mireille's eyes had gone wide, clearly remembering her encounter with the enchanted cage.

Vengeance leapt from Hawke's chest and poised at the ready, next to the cocoon.

"Vengeance will set her loose from the cage. She can help if Ilse gets out of hand."

Fiona and Jonah both said "Vengeance?" at the same time.

Alannah took a quick second to give them a brief rundown, that the enchanted spider was Hawke's cohort or accomplice or something.

"Odd" was all Fiona said.

Jonah shook his head in disbelief. "Never heard of that before."

Alannah shrugged. Neither had she before she stepped foot into this house, but now, it seemed natural to her.

Fiona and Alannah stood next to each other and cast an enchantment that rendered Ilse impotent. Vengeance released her from the cocoon but kept her hands bound and her mouth gagged.

Ilse was throwing daggers with her eyes at all of them, but nary a one gave a damn about Ilse's opinion at this stage.

She's lucky she's alive, Alannah thought. And that was gospel.

They led Ilse upstairs and left Jonah with Hawke.

"Hold on," Jonah called out to them. "Alannah. What about that?" He pointed to the spider.

Alannah resisted the shudder that rippled along her spine.

"Vengeance. Let's let Jonah do what he needs to do for Hawke. He'll take care of him. Come."

Alannah later couldn't even begin to explain what in the world made her talk to Ven as if she were a human. Or a child. Or even a pet. She was a spider; someone had tried to point that out to her.

That evidently hadn't mattered at the time.

To Alannah's imminent shock, Vengeance cast a line to the ceiling, pounced up high, and suspended mid-air, she alit on Alannah's shoulder.

Alannah could only imagine what her face must have looked like for she saw it reflected in her sister's face.

Mireille clamped her hand over her mouth, eyes wide. Then she slowly lowered her arm. "I wouldn't have believed it if anyone had ever told me. Ever."

Frozen, Alannah responded, "I know, right?"

Fiona raised her brow. "I really have seen it all, now."

Then, suddenly, an emotion flowed through Alannah. Guilt, and maybe something else. "Hey, Ven, thank you for your help earlier." She held her breath and put out her finger toward the spider, praying the hairy-legged critter wouldn't bite her.

Or worse.

Vengeance took a step forward on Alannah's shoulder, letting her side touch Alannah's finger.

Alannah softly ran her fingertip along Vengeance's

side, surprised at how velvety it was. So different than it looked.

Then with a backward glance toward the basement, she climbed the stairs, following behind Ilse, Mireille, and Fiona.

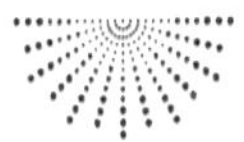

CHAPTER FIFTEEN

F iona placed Ilse against a column in the middle of the kitchen and said to Alannah, "Think your furry, little eight-legged friend can strap her to this thing so she doesn't try anything?"

Alannah glanced at Vengeance. "Would you, please?"

Vengeance raised her two front legs and began to spin out a line of her enchanted silk. The web wrapped itself around Ilse, binding her to the thick wood beam.

"Maybe remove her gag?" Fiona gave Ilse a stern look. "One misstep and I'll ask Alannah to put that gag back on you."

Alannah nodded in agreement.

It was clear from Fiona's barely contained fury that she'd not forgotten the mistreatment she'd had at Ilse's hand. How as the coven chair, Ilse had wanted to kill Fiona's falcon.

Ilse's eyes glowed red, eclipsing most of the white. "You will pay for this. My second is coming."

"Your second is dead," Alannah informed her.

"What?" If it was possible, Ilse's eyes turned even redder, the white completely gone. "She's not."

"She tried to kill me," Alannah said.

"You're not strong enough to take her out." Ilse fumed. "And you know that witches are not to kill other witches."

Anger raged in Alannah. She stormed toward Ilse and got in her face. "You do not have the right to tell me witches are not to kill other witches. Not when you had my sister abducted so you could—" Alannah had no clue what Ilse's plans were for her, but she knew for damned sure it would not have boded well for her. "You sicken me."

Fiona leaned against the far wall, studying Ilse. Alannah watched her cousin. Admiration swelled within her for her falcon/witch hybrid cousin. Fiona Forester was a part of InterForce Unit 13. She headed the latest paranormal squad. She'd been through so much in her life. And Alannah hadn't been around for most of that.

Fiona's relationship with Jonah had been rocky, mostly because of the issue of shifters and witches having children. Witches weren't supposed to be able to carry a shifter's baby, not without magic.

Fiona's mother had been a witch and had to get help

from more powerful witches not to lose Fiona while she was in her womb. Of course, when she'd lost her parents as a young one, Fiona had never been told she was born of a witch until she was older. Mae Forester, who adopted her and gave Fiona her own last name, had tried to tell Fiona that she was born of witches, but Fiona had rejected the idea until she'd lost Jonah's baby.

Hard lesson to learn, Alannah mused.

And so why was she falling for Hawke?

I'm not falling for him. It's just a... an...

Infatuation, her inner voice asked.

No.

Alannah wasn't the infatuation type. Never had been. She was the serious, do the right thing, get the job done, type. She'd never had flighty emotions for a man.

Especially not a shifter.

"Alannah?"

She looked up from the intricate carvings on the trim work above the sink next to Fiona. "Yes?"

"You weren't with us for a while, just checking."

I was down in that basement, hoping Hawke would be okay.

She couldn't be infatuated with him. And she couldn't fall for him. That just wouldn't do, now would it?

Alannah gave Fiona a smile of reassurance. "I'm fine. It's been a busy couple of days."

Mireille gave her a hug. "She's been busy trying to save me." She gave Ilse a dirty look. "No thanks to you."

"Zip it," Ilse sneered. "Quit your mewling."

Mewling. That brought to mind something Ilse had said earlier.

Prompted, Alannah just had to ask. "What did you mean, about Hawke's sister earlier, what you said. What was that about? What about his sister?"

"You don't know the witch hunter's secret?"

"Look, bitch." Alannah had her fill of Ilse's bullshit. "Until a short while ago, I had no idea he even existed, so no, I don't know about his secret, and I don't know anything about this witch hunter business."

"Oh, and here I thought he was someone special to you, from the way you two looked at each other," Ilse snapped.

Alannah couldn't help but wonder, did he really look at her differently? Or was this witch full of it. "Get on with it. What about his secret, and why's he called the witch hunter?"

"He hunts witches."

Mireille's eyes widened. "Why?"

"Witches killed his sister."

In the background, Vengeance hissed dangerously next to Alannah's ear. Alannah put a finger up to comfort her, though still a bit hesitant about trusting the arachnid.

"And you know this how?" Fiona's face was an unreadable mask.

"I was there. At the witch raid."

"You probably led it." Alannah spat the words before she could curb her tongue. Then again, she wasn't sure she wanted to guard her words. Not with this miserable excuse for a witch.

"Witch raid? What witch raid?" Mireille's tone was so innocent.

Alannah put her arm around her sister. "A practice that some of our kind—the less scrupulous ones--partake in. Raiding the settlements, towns, villages of other supernatural beings. Killing them all."

"Hey." Ilse glared at Alannah. "At least I wasn't part of the scavenger group."

Now this was a new one for Alannah. "What do you mean?"

"The group of witches that follow raiding parties, taking the ones that aren't quite dead for captives."

"Captives? What for?" Mireille probed.

"To turn them." Fiona's lips were set in a grim line. "To turn them into familiars, pets, whatever. And then to sell them to wealthier witches."

Only a transforming witch could do that.

"Scavengers have a transforming witch?" This surprised Alannah. Transforming witches were extremely powerful, and rare. She wouldn't have thought they'd have hung about with the scavengers, the scourge of witches.

Ilse shrugged.

Vengeance hissed at her.

"So what does this have to do with Hawke's sister?" Alannah was relentless. She had to know.

"Maybe she didn't die." Another shrug from Ilse.

Fiona paced the kitchen. "We should get details from Hawke. Where they were living and when, then we can round up the scavenger parties that may have taken her." She shook her head. "That's a slim, very slim possibility, you know."

"I have to tell him." Would she be able to tell him? Would he come out of this unharmed? Of course, right? She wrung her fingers, twining them. He'd live. If there were cause for concern, Jonah and Fiona wouldn't have been so calm. She whirled around, causing Fiona to startle, and asked, "You think he'll be okay?"

Fiona nodded. "I'm sure. He's a shifter. We heal faster."

"Looks like maybe you do have a crush on him," Ilse's tone was bitter.

Alannah glanced at her shoulder, ready to tell Ven to shut the stinking witch's mouth, but it was too late. Ven had already released a stream of web and it was wrapping itself around Ilse's head.

Ilse was moaning and groaning beneath the web, and Ven kept spinning, covering her entire face.

"Jesus," Mireille said. "She's going to smother her."

Alannah didn't give a shit, but as an officer of the law, she wanted Fiona to have full deniability and not ever be accused of breaking the law. "No, Ven. As much as I don't want her around either, it's not the right time for that. Plus, the Witch Court will take care of her."

Ven stopped, releasing the silky deathtrap.

Alannah turned to Fiona. "Do you think Vengeance might be one of those who was turned? She's pretty big, and seems to understand."

"Could be." Fiona shrugged. "Only a transforming witch could tell for sure. And she's the only kind of witch that could render a reversal spell."

"Great. And they're hard to find. I've never met one."

"I've never even heard of them," Mireille added.

"I know one," Fiona added. "I mean, I've met her once. For dinner at Mikhail's."

Alannah snapped her head in Fiona's direction. "You mean back when you and Jonah were together, years and years ago?" She couldn't mean recently could she? Alannah had been staying with the Romanoffs since Fiona and Jonah got together again, she'd know if there'd been another witch around.

"Nope. I mean as in last Sunday at dinner."

"Who? There's no—"

"The interim chair at Northfork came to the Romanoffs' for dinner. Her name is Desideria. Desi, they call her. She was Isabel Tiero's teacher back when she was younger, I guess, at boarding school or something. The High Court sent her to Northfork to manage matters while they appointed a new chair, what with Ilse's recent antics."

They glanced at the squirming Ilse, who no doubt was fuming at the mention of her lost power.

"Too bad Desideria isn't around. It'd be interesting to see if Vengeance was something else, before." Alannah voiced her thought out loud.

Mireille giggled. "My money says she was a vampire." She shuddered. "I'd rather not see that spell reversed."

Vengeance's eyes were going from one to another, as if she understood what they were saying. Alannah wondered if she did. Then she decided she'd rather not risk it. She didn't want to hurt Ven's feelings.

Wow. Did I just think that I don't want to hurt a spider's feelings?

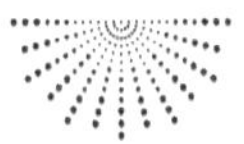

CHAPTER SIXTEEN

A few hours later, after scrounging food from Hawke's pantry for a paltry meal, Alannah washed and handed the last dish to Fiona to dry.

Alannah's mind had been on Hawke the whole time, but they'd respected boundaries and left Jonah to care for him without their interference.

"Do you think he's healed enough to hibernate? Do you know how long it will take for him to heal? He will heal, right? He's not…"

Fiona let out a soft laugh. "Slow down."

"Sorry. I guess I don't know much about this hibernating healing thing. I didn't pay close enough attention when you and Jonah… well, when all that stuff happened."

Fiona nodded. "Glad that's all in the past."

"Me, too." Alannah dried her hands on the towel then splayed it over the back of a chair to dry. "So, what do you think? You're a shifter. What can we expect?" Another thought occurred to her. "Should we take them some food?"

They wrapped two plates and covered them with foil for when the guys did come up or call out for something to eat.

Fiona put her hand on Alannah's arm. "It's not easy to kill a shifter. Magic is one way. But from what I could see, there's no danger of that. Unless there was some sort of different enchantment in the bolt she shot him with, but I doubt that. We'd know by now if she had."

Behind them, the still trussed up, blindfolded, gagged witch moved, coughing.

"Should we feed her?" Mireille asked.

"Hell no," Alannah fumed. "She's not getting food until Hawke and Jonah eat."

"So are we going to keep her like that? And what about when Hawke's better? Then what?"

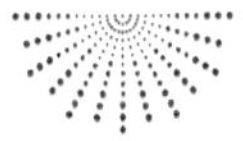

CHAPTER SEVENTEEN

Hawke was ravenous. Felt like he hadn't eaten in days. His stomach rumbled and he was sure he'd been out for at least a week. His body ached, and this bed was hard as hell.

He opened his eyes.

What the hell?

He knew that face. Jonah Romanoff. Ky's brother. What—

Hawke wanted to shake his head, to clear it. He wanted to pinch himself. *I'm not dreaming, am I?*

"Jonah?" Was that his own voice? It sounded like that of a parched man.

Jonah looked up from his phone, where he'd either been engaged in a hell of a game, or texting furiously.

"Hey, Sleeping Beauty. 'Bout time you woke up. I was getting hungry, but didn't want to leave you." As if to punctuate his statement, Jonah's stomach rumbled with hunger. Jonah laughed. "See?"

"What are you doing here?" *And where's Alannah?* He hesitated to ask, didn't want to tip his hand too much.

Would he ever stop playing things so close to the vest? Would he ever trust someone?

His bear roared an answer.

Jonah studied him. It was remarkable how much he resembled his brother Malachi.

"Mikhail sent me. I'm following up on Alannah's wild-haired idea that something was wrong with her sister. Guess it wasn't as half-baked as we thought. What are you doing?"

"Long story." Hawke pushed himself to a sitting position and leaned against the wall. He gave Jonah the briefest explanation, because frankly, he didn't want to talk.

"Ilse has been a thorn in the Romanoff family's side for a while now."

"Is she contained?" Hawke glanced about.

"The girls have her upstairs."

Hawke found his open. "Girls?"

"Alannah, Mireille, Fiona—my woman. Alannah and Fiona are cousins. Did you know?"

Hawke didn't know shit. Until recently, he hadn't even known Alannah existed. Now he couldn't imagine a day without seeing her. Even if she was a feisty redhead. Especially because she was a feisty redhead.

With an ass that doesn't quit.

All right, he pushed his bear and his hormones back.

"I didn't know they were related. Seems I don't know much about anything."

"Ky mentioned after you left the service you pretty much went off the grid."

"That sums it up." Hunting witches and housing birds of prey. That was what his life had become.

Birds of prey! Damn, how long had he been out? How were his birds? He needed to get out there and check on them. Sure, the help took care of them just fine, but Hawke didn't like not getting out there personally to see to their wellbeing.

"How long have I been out?"

"A few hours. I got you to shift so you could heal. Then you shifted back not too long ago. I figured you'd wake up shortly after that. And here you are. Hungry? It smells like someone's been cooking up there. I'll give them a shout to hook us up."

Hawke smiled. "I'm not an invalid. And it's not the first time I've tangled with a witch." He stood. Though he didn't say it out loud, this was the worst he'd ever been hurt. How the hell did that happen? It wasn't like him to let his guard down.

He replayed the events in his head. He'd intervened to save Vengeance. "Where's Vengeance?"

"Your spider? She's with Alannah. On her shoulder, the last time I saw her, when they went upstairs."

Hawke frowned. Since when did Ven have anything

to do with a witch? She hated witches just as much as he did.

Only he now found himself not hating all witches. At least, not Alannah or Mireille. And with his friend's brother Jonah being mated to a witch, maybe there was a third he didn't mind.

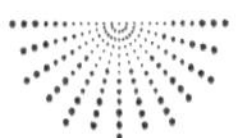

CHAPTER EIGHTEEN

Hawke couldn't sleep. It was the break of dawn. Everyone had gone to a guest room to crash after being up all night making plans and arrangements.

He was unable to catch any shut-eye. Maybe because he spent that time hibernating. Maybe because his bear was restless. Maybe because he felt like he was in an unsettled place. He padded to the kitchen in bare feet, without a shirt, figuring no one else would be around.

Ilse had been moved to the basement, set up in a cocoon. Fiona and Jonah had made arrangements for someone from the Shifter Council to pick her up and make sure she was delivered to the Witch Court to answer for her actions.

If he never saw her again, he'd be happy. He'd

almost be tempted to say if he never saw another witch again, he'd be happy.

But that would be very untrue. He couldn't push Alannah from his mind. He wanted to know everything about her. Her favorite color. Her favorite animal—he hoped that was a bear. Her favorite position—okay, maybe that was pushing it a bit. He couldn't help it, though. He had an early morning raging hard-on that wouldn't quit. The kind you wake up with that hurt so badly, the pain was exquisite and could only be quenched with pleasure.

Stifle it, he urged his bear. And his body. Damn.

This morning was weird for him. Every night since the day Vengeance had become a part of his life, she'd slept in his room.

This night, of all nights, when he'd told her he was going to his room to crash, and invited her to hop onto his shoulder, she'd turned around and cast a line to the kitchen's ceiling, then ridden that line to a shelf, where she'd backed herself into a corner, facing the basement door.

Maybe she was worried about Ilse getting loose. But that couldn't be, could it? She'd never done that with any of the other witches that he'd imprisoned in one of her cocoon cages in the basement.

He opened the fridge door and took out the milk jar and downed half of it in a few long swallows. Putting the jar back, he damned near had a stroke.

Fuck.

"What the hell? Where'd you come from?"

Alannah was in a corner, watching him, silently, her green eyes were unfathomable depths that gave nothing away.

Glowing dots on her shoulder meant one thing.

Vengeance.

I get that Ven rode on her shoulder while I was out, but what the hell? First, Ven refuses to come to my room, now she's hanging out with a witch?

Granted, a very hot witch that he'd like to get to know better, but still, what the hell? Where was the loyalty, Ven?

"I've been standing here."

"The whole time?" Now, he was ready to chastise his bear. First, Ven, now the bear doesn't even let him know there's someone else in the room. More disloyalty?

Surely you heard the heartbeat. Surely you felt her presence.

The bear was silent.

Oh, I see how it is. Gang up on Hawke day, is it?

More silence from the bear. And in the corner, lips full, eyes wide, Alannah watched him, also silent, with Vengeance's glowing eyes on him.

He didn't need to stick around for this. He knew just the place to go where he had friends. His birds.

He slipped on his shoes and grabbed a flannel shirt hanging nearby.

"I'll be back in a while."

"Wait, Hawke." Alannah's voice was barely above a whisper.

He froze, hand on the door knob.

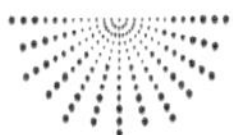

Alannah didn't know what she'd done to him. It was as if she'd pissed him off, and yet, she couldn't think of a single wrong she'd inflicted. Didn't he realize she had nothing to do with this hatred thing he had for witches? Didn't he realize she had nothing in common with the witches he believed had killed his sister?

All of these thoughts, her complete reaction to his treatment of her did nothing to diminish the flurry of emotions creating a blizzard around her.

When he walked in, no shirt, pants fitting just right, and—God forbid—she'd seen an erection outlined in those jeans, my-oh-my, what an erection that had been. In the darkness, she felt a blush heating her cheeks and fought the urge to turn away. He couldn't see that, surely. She'd heard of shifters' sensitive sight and hearing, but her blush wouldn't be visible, not in this dimness, of that she felt comfortably sure.

Sort of comfortably sure.

Vengeance was moving about on Alannah's shoulder. Her little feet lifting then dropping, though she wasn't really changing spots, more like changing positions.

Why so restless, little one, Alannah wondered.

His back was to her at the door, the flannel shirt hiding the muscles she'd seen before. She thought of the other things his shirt hid. A chest that was broad, muscular, and remarkably sparse of hair.

Lickable, as her friends would have said.

Very lickable, Alannah agreed with her own assessment.

And arms, too, nice thick arms that could hold a woman securely.

She bit back the sigh that threatened. *What's the point of being infatuated with a guy that seems to hate your guts right about now? A guy who dislikes you so much, he's running off into the daybreak.*

Still, she owed Vengeance this. Because deep down, Alannah couldn't shake the idea that Vengeance hadn't been born a spider. And she wanted to take her with her to New York to have this Desideria take a look at her, maybe even check her to see if she was something else.

He was waiting. She'd asked him to wait. Had done

it for Vengeance, though Ven didn't even know what Alannah was up to.

"What's up?" He raised a brow and asked when she didn't immediately tell him why she'd asked him to wait.

"I was hoping to talk to you."

He shuffled his feet as if unsure what to say. "I'll be back later, if it can wait."

She didn't want to wait. Later, there would be others around. Later she might lose her nerve. Later— "Maybe I could join you?" Did she really just ask him that? She had no clue where he was going or what he would be doing. And he was the witch hunter, after all.

He frowned. "It's cold out there. And I—"

"Please."

He didn't say a word. Took a hoodie off the hook by the door. "Put this on. It'll keep you warm and protect Vengeance. Since I'm figuring she's coming along."

Alannah glanced at the spider. She supposed Vengeance was, she hadn't really given it much thought, assuming that perhaps the spider would sit on the perch she'd been on when Alannah first walked into the kitchen a couple of hours ago.

She took the hoodie from his hand, careful not to let their fingers touch. Goodness knew, she didn't need that, not in her heightened state of awareness to his sexiness.

Vengeance leapt from her shoulder to his and Alannah pulled the hoodie over her head, releasing her hair. No sooner had she done that, Ven jumped back onto her shoulder.

Alannah glanced at Hawke to gauge his reaction. His face was immobile. A statue had more emotion than he did. She was going to apologize but realized how silly it would sound. What was she to say?

I'm sorry your spider seems to like me better today.

Yeah, not.

"Ready?" His voice was huskier than a moment ago, and it made an undercurrent run through her that left her weak in the knees.

She felt Vengeance making her way across her shoulder and onto her back, then into the hood as if it was something she regularly did.

She wanted to ask what they were going to do, but never got a chance. Before she knew it, the door was open and he was ushering her outside, closing it behind them with a slight click that wouldn't disturb anyone inside.

Moments later, they were heading toward a shed on the side of the property, the ground crunching beneath them slightly with the slight snowfall that had graced the fields the night before. The sun was just rising, creating a sparkle in the white snow, making the scenery surreally beautiful. She breathed out in amazement at the beauty before them.

"I see why you like it here," she told him, her breath left light puffs in the cooler temperatures.

He glanced sideways at her as he pulled the door of

the shed wide and sat on a four-wheel all terrain type of vehicle.

Where are we going?

She didn't get to ask, the roar of the engine filled the air. He jumped off and closed the shed door, then resumed his spot on the vehicle and looked at her expectantly. "Well?"

She nodded and climbed on behind him.

With a lurch that made her gasp, he took off. She would've wondered if that was on purpose. This was the time for kneejerk reactions and quick reflexes.

She grabbed him, wrapping her arms around him, pulling up close to him, before she could be ditched.

And that was a bit of a mistake. Oh yes, quite the mistake.

Feeling the warmth of his body heat against the front of her, the muscles beneath her fingertips that were flexing and unflexing with every turn.

They flew through paths and trees, darting left and right.

Yes, very definitely not a good thing to be this close to him, but in so many ways, it was just the right thing. It had been a long time since she'd had her hands on a man, and never, ever, a man like this.

The scent of him the wind blew into her nostrils was earthy, sexy, woodsy, mixed with what might have been a hint of cinnamon.

How is a man like this single?

That was her first thought.

Her second thought was: *Because he's a killer of witches and it seems it'd be hard to maintain a relationship when you have to explain that there's a big ass spider that locks women in magical cages in your basement.*

True, that'd be hard to explain.

Outside a large fenced in area, he pulled into a pebble-covered parking lot. She glanced around but there was no signage to indicate where they were. On her back, Vengeance was shuffling, seeming to be digging deeper into the hoodie's hood.

Hawke jumped off and gave her a hand to dismount.

Maybe he doesn't hate me as much as I thought.

He pulled a set of keys out and unlocked a padlock on the twelve-foot high gate, matching the height of the fencing that enclosed the area as far as she could see into the wooded area.

"Watch yo—"

A screech interrupted Hawke. A shadow rocketed toward them. Unsure what was happening, Alannah dipped low and covered her head with her hands.

When Hawke laughed, she raised her head. The largest falcon she'd ever seen was perched on his arm. "Is it safe?"

That got another laugh from Hawke. "Jester, meet Alannah."

The raptor turned his head then angled it, his eyes piercing her.

"Are you sure he doesn't think I'm breakfast?" She

wished she could control the shaking in her voice, but hell, she thought she was going to get scalped, at the very least.

"No. He doesn't typically attack humans."

She stepped closer, and felt Vengeance shuffling around in the hood. "Would he hurt your spider?"

"I don't think Vengeance wants to give him a shot. She always hides in the hood. Though lately, it seems she's made a new friend in you."

Alannah grimaced. "Would you believe me if I told you that I used to hate spiders?"

Hawke smiled. "I'd say it was clear from the way you shuddered the first dozen times you saw her."

"Oh." Alannah clapped a hand over her mouth, feeling guilty, because what if Ven really was a human or a shifter under that spider skin. "Say, you're quite the beast whisperer, aren't you? Spiders and this falcon. Is that why they call you Hawke?"

"No. My surname really is Hawke. My mother was a falcon shifter. A bit ironic, wouldn't you say. And now, here I am, with falcons."

"Plural? There are more than one?"

As if to answer that question, another falcon circled around them lazily, soaring and shrieking. "That's Erethra. She's ready for Jester to give up his spot so she can visit."

"Are they friendly? Why do you have them? Are they pets?"

"Pets?" He frowned. "Hardly. They come here when

they're wounded. Just show up. Sometimes not wounded, even. And they stay as long as they want. Until they leave."

"How many are there? Do they ever leave?"

"A dozen, give or take. Not forever, they don't. They might vanish, but they usually bring another one back with them."

"So, they aren't found hurt in the forest by people and brought to you?"

"I've had that happen with one or two, but most of them just show up or are brought by others."

The bird made a soft sound and cocked his head, appraising Alannah.

"Hi, Jester. You're a handsome fella, now, aren't you? Can I touch him?"

Hawke shrugged. "I'd say do it at your own peril. They've never attacked a human."

She put her hand out. Jester brought his hooked wicked-looking beak close, then tilted his head. She ran her finger over the smooth feathers on top.

"Do they ever see any other humans? Other than you, I mean."

"I have a couple of guys that help me, that way if I miss a visit, the birds get whatever they need."

"This is incredible."

"Put your arm out. Here, parallel to mine."

She did, and swiftly, Jester hopped on over. His talons squeezing but not digging in.

"I'd have thought this would hurt."

"He seems to get it. They all do. It's as if they know they could hurt us, and they spare us." He smiled a crooked sexy smile that made her heart melt.

She tried not to stare at his mouth, but when she looked at his eyes, she felt like she was being sucked into a place she didn't ever want to leave.

The shadow above moved in a different pattern, and in a split second, Erethra had taken Jester's spot.

"This is Erethra. She's the queen of the roost."

The falcon on his hand shook her feathers, then splayed her wings, flapping majestically.

"See. She agrees." Hawke smiled at the falcon.

Alannah melted. This man would be way too easy to fall in love with. She needed to get out of Russia quickly.

"What?" he asked.

"Nothing." She shook her head. As if she'd tell him how damned hard he was to resist.

"Something put that expression on your face."

Time to switch subjects. "Actually, there was something I wanted to discuss with you."

She told him about the raids, the scavengers, the transformation spells, and how she had a feeling Vengeance might be one of those who had this done to her.

"You think so?" It looked like he was still trying to process this all. "And you think maybe my sister wasn't killed?"

Hawke knew hope was a dangerous thing. It could lead him down a path where he'd actually believe there was a chance Renee wasn't dead.

Fuck.

That would be the end all, be all of his dreams achieved, having his sister alive.

He looked off into the horizon. "It can't be. It would be so amazing." He muttered the words and realized he'd said them out loud. He'd have a new focus. He wouldn't hunt witches. He'd renew and put all his energies into researching that raid, into finding who and where any live captives were taken, into finding who participated in the raid and what information they had.

"Hawke?"

He glanced at the woman who'd come to mean so

much to him in such a short time and realized he'd been in his own world and not talking to her. Clearly she'd asked him something.

"Sorry. What?"

"Did you hear what I said about Vengeance?"

"What's that?"

"About taking her to New York, to see Desideria. To find out if it's possible that she's a human or even a shifter, or who knows, maybe a witch."

That would mean I wouldn't have her with me anymore.

Vengeance had been the closest thing to a best friend he'd had all these years.

Then again, it'd be mighty shitty and selfish to keep her prisoner in a spider's body if that's not who Vengeance was. He figured Vengeance was a female, though he had no idea what made him think so.

"Yeah, I don't want to be unfair to Vengeance, but I'd sure like to find out about my sister. Going to the United States would throw that schedule off. Our family was living in Europe when—" He didn't want to say the words out loud. "—when my family was attacked."

Ven might prefer to live with her, not me.

Now why did that make him sad? Why was he sad over a hairy legged little—maybe not so little—spider?

"Let's have Jonah ask Mikhail if Desideria can visit. Then you don't have to leave."

"Jester, Erethra, why don't you two give us a few

moments of privacy. Plus, her arm's probably about numb from holding it up."

The birds flew away.

Alannah gasped.

"What's wrong?"

"It's not normal. What just happened isn't normal."

"What do you mean?"

"You just told them to leave. And they did. As if they understood."

"Maybe you're right. Maybe I am a beast whisperer." He laughed at that joke. "Alannah, I have a favor to ask you. You have every right to say no, considering what I put you and your sister through."

In the rising sun's rays, her green eyes were iridescent, her hair glinted as if on fire. "What?"

"It would be a lot of help if I had a witch on my side while I'm trying to learn more about the raid on my family, and maybe what might have happened to my sister, if she was taken, or if she died." *Plus, I can't imagine not having you in my life, daily.*

She studied him, and on her shoulder, Vengeance appeared, hiding under the cover of her burnished copper hair, spindly legs twitching as she settled into a comfortable spot near the crook of her neck. "Well—" She took a deep breath. "I mean…"

He regretted asking. He put her in an awkward position. Clearly, she wanted to decline.

"I shouldn't have asked." He kicked at the dirt and

snow with his shoe. He was such a fool. What made him think she'd want to traipse throughout Europe looking for answers for the guy who kidnapped her and her sister. "I'm sure you have enough to do."

What does she do, anyway? It occurred to him he had a lot to learn about this woman. If she'd give him a chance. Which right now, it didn't look like she would.

"I'm in between jobs." She grimaced. "Maybe in between guilds. I was in the same guild as Ilse. I'm sure after the fiasco, they're probably assessing if they should dissolve the guild."

He understood covens, he got that a coven was a band of witches, but what the hell was a guild? "Guild?"

"A group of covens organized into a guild. For protection, education. That sort of thing."

"I get that. We shifters do clans."

"You don't seem to have a clan."

He shook his head. "I've been solo since my family was taken." He didn't want to go into all the different things he'd gone through. How difficult it was to trust or be a part of something that could be snatched away at a moment's notice.

"How about some coffee?" Hawke pointed toward a small cottage in the corner.

Inside the little house, he set up a pot to brew.

"Would you ever consider being a part of something?" She leaned against the table, looking just like she belonged there.

If that something included you. "I'd consider it."

"I'll help you."

You could have knocked Hawke down with a feather, that's how much her statement caught him off-guard.

CHAPTER TWENTY-ONE

Alannah couldn't have said why she said what she did. Out of the blue, she'd blurted that she'd help him. At first, she stood absorbing the words, and trying to absorb the fact she was the one who voiced them. That really was her. It was. And she did say it.

It was his eyes. It was that tortured look deep in his eyes, and when a flicker of a silver-white flame gleamed in those blue depths. It was as if something within him was calling to her soul.

Here she was, in this cottage, not much more than a shack, with this gorgeous man she'd only recently met, and not under the best of circumstances, and she couldn't imagine not being next to him. She couldn't see a day where she didn't get to be near him.

I guess if that's the only way I can have him near me, by helping him with his cause, then I'll take that.

And maybe she'd get over him during that time. She'd see the imperfections she always found in men, and she'd not be intrigued or interested in him.

Not likely.

It was evident, she wasn't the only one stunned as he stood, speechless, staring at her.

She felt a slight tickle against her neck as Vengeance stepped out from under her hair and shot a line of web to the ceiling, then swung away and into a cubby hole at the top of the ceiling, hidden out of sight.

Odd, Alannah thought, but she didn't get much time to think on it. Hawke had closed the distance between them. Her breath hitched as he leaned closer. His breath was hot on her cheek, and his body warmth, all those muscles, it was like standing next to a furnace.

Or maybe that's my damned hormones, because it's been so long.

She tried to dismiss her reaction to the sexy man standing so close to her, yet not touching her.

A myriad of emotions shook her. She ached inside, wondering what it would be like to have those large, capable hands on her body, to have those lips against hers, or in other areas.

She didn't realize she sighed out loud until she heard the small breathless sound escape between her lips.

His eyes held hers on lockdown, daring her to move. The only move she wanted was to jump into his arms, wrap her legs around him and never let him go.

God, when did I turn into THAT woman.

Right after I met him, she surmised.

His hands rose, swiftly, clutching the back of her head, holding her captive while he swooped in and claimed her mouth.

The man knew how to kiss. Her skin seared where it touched his, her nerve endings tingled, and she was going to fall if she didn't hold onto something.

Her hands knew exactly what she needed to hold onto, for they reached out as if on their own volition and walked her fingers up his chest until she'd reached that magnificently muscled thick neck of his. She wrapped her hands around, and wound them into his hair, scoring his scalp with her nails.

He gave as good as he got, though, thrusting his tongue in, tangling it with hers in a dance that was primeval and graceful.

She leaned against him, her toes curled in her shoes, her mouth groaned into his.

She pressed her body against his, the launch sequence in motion, fully activated. She felt his reaction against her body, and held her breath, thinking of the imprint of the hardness she'd seen in his pants earlier.

Heaven help me, the things I could do with that.

His tongue traced her lips and shivers erupted across her flesh from head to toe.

"Hawke," she breathed his name out, her eyes beginning to drop in full supplication. She wanted nothing more than to join with this man.

How did we go from zero to sixty so fast?

He pulled back. "Don't worry," his voice was sex-husky. "I won't push you."

I wish you would.

CHAPTER TWENTY-TWO

Somewhere in the middle of the ride back to Hawke's home, Alannah noticed they weren't alone, not exactly, anyway.

Behind and above, Erethra and Jester flew, as if sentries.

That wasn't such a big deal, but when a large shadow crossed over the four-wheeler, it drew Alannah's attention.

She glanced up again, then tugged on Hawke's sleeve. When he slowed and looked back at her, she pointed up.

More than a dozen falcons in varying sizes were following them.

He shrugged, but didn't seem to think much of it as he picked up speed again.

Alannah's legs were still shaking when Hawke pulled the four-wheeler into the driveway of his home, her lips still swollen from that kiss, her heart still racing. She dismounted and felt Vengeance making her way out of the hood and onto her shoulder.

She'd really agreed to help him. She had. She actually had. And they'd kissed.

And damn. What a kiss.

Hawke secured the vehicle, then pulled the shed door shut.

Then he froze, staring.

The SUV that Fiona and Jonah had come in was there, but so was another vehicle. A black Mercedes sedan with dark tinted windows. Alannah wasn't much for cars, but this one didn't look cheap. And it was spotless, even though it had come all the way out here in the country.

She glanced at Hawke to see if he might know the car. "Friend of yours?"

He shook his head. "Nope."

A knot formed in the pit of her stomach. Alannah braced herself. "I hope everything is okay." She lowered, ready to run in.

Hawke put a hand on her arm. "Hold on. Element of surprise, maybe they didn't hear us approach. It's not the main way in. Let's go around the back."

She nodded. "Good call" and followed him through the field, picking their way carefully among the snow and vegetation, keeping the footfalls to a minimum silence.

"I'm ready to shift, if needed," he whispered.

He didn't have to say it. Mireille, Fiona, and Jonah were in there.

"And I'm ready to do my thing."

"Ven, be on guard," he told the spider.

Alannah felt the spider shuffling on her shoulder.

At the back door, laughter came from inside. Some of it unmistakably from Mireille and Fiona.

Alannah looked at Hawke. "I don't think it's a dangerous situation."

"Agreed." He pushed the back door open.

Jonah, Fiona, and Mireille turned their way. Two men Alannah didn't recognize stood next to them.

"It's about time." Mireille gave them a mock frown. "If I hadn't thought you were with Hawke, I'd have been worried."

"Sorry." Alannah tried to look apologetic, though she didn't regret the way the morning had gone.

Hawke's eyes were glued on the newcomers. "I don't think I've had the pleasure." His tone was guarded.

Jonah stepped forward. "Mikhail texted that Desideria couldn't make it." Then he frowned. "Maybe you don't know what I'm talking about," he said as if it just occurred to him that perhaps Hawke had no idea of the girls' discussion yesterday while he was out.

"Is this about that transformation stuff Alannah mentioned this morning?" He glanced at Vengeance. "For Ven?"

Meanwhile, Alannah also stared. Two tall men with

dark skin the hue of mahogany and light colored eyes with gold flecks.

Wizards, her witch instinct told her. These two were her kind.

But she'd never seen them before and the power that emanated from them was almost tangible. They released a golden aura she wasn't sure anyone who wasn't a witch or a wizard could see.

With their wide chests, muscular arms, and strong jawlines, Alannah couldn't help but stare. They were identical.

Twin wizards was a rarity. In truth, she'd heard there'd only been one other instance, and that was during the medieval times.

Jonah cleared his throat, and Alannah realized she was staring as was Hawke. "Meet Cedric. And Jenner."

Alannah bit back a gasp. She'd heard those names. Probably every witch in existence had.

The dark-skinned men with their amber colored eyes nodded their greetings.

Hawke's stare had not subsided, nor had a smile appeared on his face. Instead, a frown creased his forehead. He turned to Jonah. "You know they are…"

It was as if he didn't want to say it.

"Wizards," the two newcomers said simultaneously. Their voices sounded as if they were in an echo chamber.

Eerie.

Mireille was practically drooling. Alannah understood why, they were remarkable looking, striking, with that skin so dark and gleaming, and those eyes, amber and glowing. Not to mention their high cheekbones and regal bearing. Closely cropped ebony hair crowned their heads while jeans and turtlenecks covered their forms. She had a feeling they'd look as comfortable in long ceremonial robes.

"They aren't just any wizards," Fiona added, her voice reverential. "They're part of the Circle."

"Everyone's heard of them," Mireille seemed to have found her voice.

"I suppose I don't know the right people," Hawke said. "What can I do for you?"

The way he said it sounded more like he was saying, what the hell do you want?

Jenner tipped his head slightly to the left, looked at Fiona and Jonah, then said, "As we were saying before you walked in, Desideria couldn't make it. She said there might be a need for some assistance. She called us, as we are the ones who are closest who might be able to help."

Just that moment, as if she'd been beckoned, Vengeance skittered across Alannah's shoulder and down her bicep, toward her forearm.

Cedric smiled at the spider. "You're quite the formidable one, aren't you?" He held his hand out, his fingers almost touching Alannah's.

Vengeance sidestepped across Alannah's arm, down

the top of her hand, and took a long leap onto Cedric's arm.

Alannah couldn't have held her gasp back. She didn't realize she'd reached for Hawke's hand until she felt the warmth of his fingers holding hers. She squeezed hard. "I was right," she whispered. "I'm sure of it."

"Could we have a moment?" Cedric asked.

"A moment alone. Privacy," Jenner clarified.

In her hand, Hawke's fingers stiffened. She squeezed again, and leaned into him. "You have to trust someone, sometime."

The look his eyes gave her brought back the kiss. A flush rose from her chest, heating her face.

"I do trust someone." His voice was so low, she barely heard the words, but what it did to her body was like a tsunami roaring in her mind, coursing through her. Hawke turned to Jenner and Cedric. He pointed to the side. "You can use the dining area."

They left the room, and Alannah prayed all would turn out okay for Vengeance.

She didn't want to eavesdrop or be nosy, but she couldn't help but see in the cabinet's glass in the hallway. It gave her a perfect view of the dining area Jenner and Cedric had just entered.

Amber light flared from Jenner's hands, resting over him and Vengeance like a halo.

A flash of brightness forced Alannah's eyes closed, and even then, behind drawn lids, she still saw tiny sparks. She rubbed her eyes to clear them, then opened them once more. The tiny points of light had become smaller, almost like the ones that appeared whenever she stood too quickly.

She blinked them away.

Jenner and Cedric exited the dining area, and behind them was a young woman. She had dark brown hair and light blue eyes, and her cheek was marked with a half-moon crescent scar, a white mark that spanned an inch of her high set cheekbones.

Her hair was pulled back and she had the tablecloth from Hawke's dining room table wrapped around her.

Hawke was transfixed. His fingers had gone from stiff to limp. He stared at the new arrival as if she were a ghost.

Hawke's hand fell out of Alannah's and he approached the dark-haired young woman.

"You." He touched a finger to the scar on her cheek. "You were Vengeance. All this time?"

She nodded. Then she burst into the longest most mournful wail Alannah had ever heard.

He wrapped his arms around the young woman then locked eyes with Alannah.

One word left his lips.

"Renee."

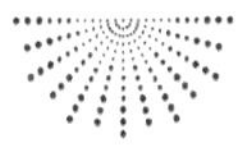

Hawke was numb. This was Renee. All this time. He put his mouth close to her ear. "All this time, you were Vengeance?"

She nodded, her body tiny against his.

"My baby sister. They didn't kill you?"

"No. I was turned and then one day they gave me to you."

"Ah, God." He hugged her tighter. "Damn them. I'll kill them all."

She turned eyes that matched his toward his face and locked gazes with him.

"Terrence. No."

"What?" He was shocked. Did she not want revenge?

"I can't do the killing anymore. I need peace. I need to be..." She inhaled, then released the word with a sob. "...me."

"Aw, damn." His urge for revenge vanished like a deflating balloon. His little sister needed him.

He looked up at the two men who'd given her back to him.

"Thank you," he mouthed.

They nodded, all seriousness. "She will need rest. A lot of it. Though she's no longer under enchantment, the reversal spell isn't easy on a body."

"Got it." Hawke would give his sister all the recuperation time she needed. Right here.

Renee put her hands on his cheeks. "There's something you need to know."

"Erethra, Jester, and the rest of your gang—"

"I'd never have let them hurt you." He took in her serious expression. "Ever."

"It's not that."

"Then…"

Renee reached out and took Alannah's hand. "You were right. All along, you knew I was not a spider." Tears glistened in Renee's eyes.

Alannah sniffed and wiped away a tear of her own. "I'm so glad you're okay. And thank you…"

"No, thank you." Renee hugged her. "And Jester, Erethra, and the others, they are the same as I was."

Jenner and Cedric again spoke at the same moment. "What is this?"

"I have an aviary, with falcons."

"Actually," Alannah interjected. "They followed us here. They're in the trees. Well, they were. They should still be there. Do you think you could look at them? Help them if need be?"

"What about the witch downstairs?" Renee asked.

"She can keep for now." Cedric said. At least, Hawke thought it was Cedric.

CHAPTER TWENTY-FOUR

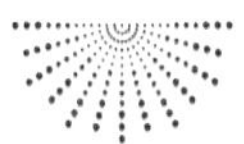

Alannah was on Hawke's porch, bundled against the chill, sitting on the rocker. Next to her, Mireille and Renee sat in a glider, wide enough for two, wrapped and tucked under a shared blanket. Across from them, not far from the shed that housed the four-wheeler, was a barn, smaller and much newer than the house. Hawke said he had it built right after he acquired the property.

Jonah and Fiona were inside at the kitchen table, on the phone with Mikhail and their InterForce Unit. Contacting the Shifter Council, and the Witch Court was also on their list of things to do.

Making a pot of hot cocoa—Hawke didn't have marshmallows, which she told him with a smile that he'd have to rectify—Alannah had served each, Mireille and Renee, and then set mugs out for Jonah and Fiona.

She prepped three extra cups for Hawke, Jenner, and Cedric for when they came back inside.

Jenner and Cedric had taken one look at the falcons that had followed Alannah and Hawke from the aviary and confirmed that indeed, these falcons had been transformed.

Alannah had held back a gasp, barely capturing it. The shock of knowing so many individuals had been transformed…

"Can you help?" Hawke asked Cedric and Jenner.

They nodded.

Hawke had assembled an assortment of clothing and blankets as well as heaters and gone toward the barn.

Fiona had grumbled about how InterForce needed to be brought in to handle the scavengers and then she and Jonah had adjourned to the kitchen, satellite phones and laptops at the ready.

Now, Alannah sat on the porch, watching all the falcons in the trees, majestic and patient. Hawke would come out every few minutes and another falcon would land on his arm and he'd go into the barn.

One by one, the falcons went in, but no one came out, except Hawke to get another falcon.

It was a nail-biting occasion for Alannah. One she didn't relish for Hawke, wondering what was going on in there, but glad she wasn't in attendance.

She listened into Mireille and Renee's chatter, trying to keep her mind off the ordeal in the barn.

When they fell silent, she glanced at them. They were looking at a spider building a web in the juncture of the porch's railing.

Alannah noticed for the first time, she didn't shudder at seeing a spider. Renee's expression was somber.

"Are you okay?" Alannah was concerned for Renee, wondering what was on her mind.

Renee nodded, but her eyes glistened with tears. One tear escaped and made its way down her cheek, slowly, cascading over the moon-shaped scar.

"I'm sorry." Renee's lower lip trembled.

"What for?" Mireille took Renee's hand in hers, holding it, squeezing it gently.

"I took you captive. I put you in that cage. You were burned." She sobbed softly. "And you," she said to Alannah. "I was not kind to you either."

Alannah left her chair and joined the two of them. Squishing between them on the glider, she hugged Renee. "You were doing what was right at the moment. It's not like we didn't attack back." She smiled, hoping to pull Renee from the despair she seemed to be sinking into.

"Thank you." Renee swiped at tears in her eyes. "I'm so thankful that you… I know Ilse is a bitch, but I'm so glad she brought us together."

The door to the barn opened, Hawke strode out, empty handed. Broad shoulders carried proudly, head held high. He was in his element, and this was the happiest she'd seen him. She could tell, even from this distance without seeing a smile on his face.

Alannah thought of that man in the barn that had come to mean so much to her.

Renee sniffled, her eyes following Alannah's as she watched Hawke take another raptor into the barn.

"You care for him."

"I—" Alannah didn't know how to answer. Didn't want to answer. How could she even begin to explain feelings she was still wrapping her head around herself?

Renee's piercing gaze shot straight to Alannah's core.

She's just like her brother, in that.

"Don't deny. I'm a shifter. I can hear your heart speed up when you look at him."

Warmth rose up Alannah's neck to her face despite the cool weather. She released a sigh. "I care for him."

"I was there in the cottage at the aviary," Renee reminded her. "Remember the spider in the corner?"

The warmth turn to a searing heat as Alannah remembered the kiss and the fact that Vengeance had been watching. She turned her face away to keep the telltale blush from making things worse for her.

Renee put her arm around her. "I've been with my brother for years. I've never seen him as alive, as happy, as I see him with you."

Alannah turned toward Renee, studied her face. Did

Renee really see a different Hawke? Could that be because of her? She wasn't sure if she agreed.

"Let's talk about something else." Alannah wanted the focus taken off her. Now.

"Let's talk about the Circle," Mireille said.

Alannah snapped her head toward her sister. "Don't you mean you'd like to talk about our two guests?"

It was Mireille's turn to blush. "Well, if I had to say that, I'd simply say Jenner, not necessarily both of them."

"How can you even tell them apart? They're identical."

"They are not," Mireille argued.

Fiona popped her head out the door. "They are identical twins."

"They don't look the same to me," Mireille stood her ground.

"So what about Jenner?" Renee asked.

"Nothing." Mireille clammed up.

"He's in the Circle," Alannah reminded her. "They don't consort with average witches. They have their own group of elite."

Mireille shrugged. "One more." She pointed to the barn door where Hawke was coming out to collect another falcon. "Two left."

Alannah looked at the trees. Indeed, there were only two falcons waiting.

Two. She wondered what it was like in the barn.

What kind of people had been falcons? Were they all shifters? Or were they also witches and wizards?

The wait wasn't much longer.

Hawke, Jenner, Cedric, and a few more than a dozen men and women came out of the barn. Hawke was beaming. Renee jumped up from the glider and ran to her brother, hugging him. The assortment of individuals behind Hawke were talking and gesturing excitedly. They stood outside the barn, while Hawke headed toward the porch.

Tears streamed down Alannah's face. Such a miracle to behold, so many imprisoned in falcon bodies.

She hated her own kind at that moment, disgusted that witches would do this to other supernatural beings.

Off to the side, Jenner and Cedric kept to themselves, walking toward the house.

Fiona and Jonah stepped out the door at that precise moment.

"Good timing," Alannah told them. "Seems they're done."

"Every single one, a shifter," Hawke said. "Every. Single. Damned. One."

"I'm sorry," Alannah whispered under her breath, figuring he wouldn't hear her, but still sad that her kind had done this.

"It's not your fault." Hawke stepped onto the porch.

She should have known he would have heard: super sensitive hearing and all that.

Jonah clapped him on the back, pulled him into a shoulder hug. "You've done a good thing, man. A very good thing."

"It's been years. Years." Hawke's jaw was clenched with anger. "They don't know where their families are, if they're still alive, they have no money, they have nothing." He shook his head in disbelief.

"We've been on the phone with the Shifter Council and the Witch Court, as well as Mikhail and Inter-Force. We've got a solution for where they can stay, not far from here."

"I can take care of some long term, I'm sure. I need to do some thinking," Hawke said.

"We'll shuttle them to the health resort we've booked nearby, for now," Jonah told him.

"Health resort?" Hawke frowned.

"It's the best we could do and still keep them nearby. It's the closest thing to a hotel," Jonah explained.

"It looks more like a Bed & Breakfast," Fiona elaborated. "They'll enjoy it."

"Sounds like a place I should visit," Renee added with a laugh. "Especially if they offer massages."

Hawke put his arm around her. "Not a chance. I'm not letting you out of my sight."

Renee pouted, but it was clear she was happy with her brother's announcement.

Cedric and Jenner joined them on the porch. One of them was putting a phone away. Alannah guessed it was Cedric because her sister was staring at the other one.

"The Witch Court said they'd been in touch with Fiona. That we're to take Ilse with us."

"Works for me," Hawke said. "I want her out of my house and life. Forever."

"What he said," Renee concurred with her big brother.

Hawke lanced Alannah with that look, the one that made her feel like the only thing in his world. "Perhaps we could talk later?"

He probably wants to tell me I was right. That he doesn't need my help anymore.

CHAPTER TWENTY-FIVE

Jenner and Cedric had driven off, a gagged and squirming Ilse in the back seat of their car.

Alannah would be happy if she never saw that witch again. Mireille and Renee were out in the field near the barn, talking with animated hand movements and lots of laugher. Alannah had never seen Mireille bond with anyone the way she did with Renee.

Alannah and Hawke were on the porch, sitting in the glider, the world around them quiet except for the occasional giggle that drifted their way from their sisters. Alannah couldn't help fidgeting because she had this feeling Hawke wanted to talk to her so he could break it to her gently.

God, just get it over with. Rip the bandage off, already.

Hawke cleared his throat.

Here we go. She braced herself.

"Our sisters are close."

Talk about throwing her a curveball. What the heck was that about? Casual conversation? Okay, she could give as well as she got, but she'd drive the subject back to where she was sure he wanted to take it.

"They seem to be doing well together." She agreed, then added, "You don't have a mission anymore, now that your sister is here, you don't have to hunt for her, or find out what happened to her."

"True."

That hurt. He'd just agreed with her.

"And you have all those shifters. They gravitated to your aviary for a reason, I'm sure."

"It's not exactly an accident." His lips were a thin line, his brows drawn down. "Jester is actually someone I know. He's my second cousin. He was taken in the same raid Renee was."

"Unbelievable. And he found you."

"He and several others, it seems."

"What are they doing? What will you do with them?"

"Short term or long term?" His laugh was strained.

"Either, both?" she asked.

"Short term, as you heard, Fiona and Jonah are helping with accommodations."

"And long term?"

"I wanted to talk to you about it first. But maybe, it looks like I have some building to do on the property. A few cabins. Luckily the guys are strapping."

"Luckily. So, it's safe to say you don't need me

anymore. I mean, since there are no missing family members to find or answers to seek." *God, that hurt to say.*

"You're wrong. I need you more than ever. You can't tear our sisters apart. They need each other. Renee needs someone. She's attached to Mireille and you. The shifters…"

But he wasn't saying the magic words. She couldn't stay for Renee and the shifters. She'd thought initially that she could. That she'd do anything just to be around him. Now she knew that wasn't the case. If she couldn't have him, she couldn't be around him.

One day he'd find someone, and Alannah would be there, on the sidelines, watching him with whomever he found. She looked over the field. Out there, the aviary stood a short drive away. The other direction, Moscow. And she hated this place, so why did it bother her? Why did it feel like she wanted to cry because she'd just lost—everything.

"Alannah." His voice was soft. "I have a hard time saying things."

She nodded, still unable to look at him.

"No, please, look at me. Look." She turned toward him, memorizing his every feature, though she knew she'd never forget him.

His gaze was mesmerizing, pulling her into a place unlike she'd ever been, a place where passion collided with desire and exploded with a fierce and over-whelming need.

"Stop looking at me like that," she whispered, her voice hoarse as if belonging to a sexy stranger. *Stop making me want you more than I already do. Stop making me fall in love with you more than I already have.*

Her eyelids fluttered shut, a defense against the look in his eyes that was pulling her deeper and deeper.

He was leaning closer. She didn't need to open her eyes to know. She could smell the scent of him, all male, all sexy.

His lips were soft and warm, but at the same time, commanding and firm.

His tongue traced her bottom lip, then pushed its way in, claiming hers. His fingers tangled in her hair, pulling her head back, exposing her neck. His tongue abandoned its quest as it traveled the column of her throat, leaving goose bumps and tremors.

Alannah fisted her hands against the desire to release the savagery in her that was boiling to come out. She squeezed her eyes tightly against her passions.

This is pointless, isn't it? It won't go anywhere.

And yet, a part of her urged her to claim this moment and take it for all she could and treasure the memory forever. If she couldn't have him, at least she could have this.

She unfisted her hands and wound them around his neck, pulling him down. Her tongue sought his, seeking the promise of passion that he offered.

His tongue took over, dipping inside, exploring,

conquering. Her legs grew weak when his hands dropped to her ass and pulled her against his body.

"What you do to me, woman." His voice had a husky sexy quality.

She breathed out slowly, fighting to gain control of the wild horses her emotions had become.

Hawke pulled away, studied her. In the depths of his eyes, a silver flame made its presence known. "There's someone I want to introduce you to."

She gave him a look. *Now what?* She'd had so many surprises since she'd come to Russia, she wasn't sure she could handle anymore. "Okay," she said tentatively.

"Come on." He took his jacket off and put it over her shoulders, then took her hand, his large one completely enveloping hers.

HAWKE HAD TO INTRODUCE HER TO HIS BEAR. IT WAS ONE thing to have her embrace his kiss and his feelings for her, it was something else completely for her to meet his bear. He pulled her into the woods, into the thickest part of the forest, where they'd be able to have privacy.

This woman, this beautiful, curvaceous, redhaired green-eyed spitfire. This woman had to be his. She had to accept his bear.

Hawke called his bear forward, embracing and ready to endure the discomfort of the shift. The bear was eager, more than eager, and gave Hawke no chance to prepare himself for the morph. His bones creaked, the sound as painful as it was loud. The elongating had begun.

Alannah's eyes grew wide.

"It's okay," Hawke assured her, his voice a low growl as his bear was beginning to take over.

His thick white fur began to emerge while his skull widened and lengthened. His teeth grew, sharp and lethal. He shook his bear head, dug his claws into the dirt as he threw his head back and roared.

Alannah stood her ground.

And when his bear rose to his hind legs, revealing the majesty of his size, she didn't flinch.

Instead, Alannah looked into his eyes, her emerald ones gleaming with an emotion he hoped was love. She put both hands on his muzzle and studied his bear face.

"Nice to meet you." She ran her fingertips over his bear face, down his neck, to his paw.

Hawke dropped to all fours, nuzzled her with his head while she wrapped an arm around his neck.

Before he realized, he'd lain on the ground and she'd leaned against him, letting his warmth keep her from being cold.

They sat in silence, their spirits communing until Hawke could stand it no more. He had to take his body back and hold her the way he wanted to.

He morphed from his bear form, his clothes now a wrinkled mess. She was still against him while he held her.

"What do you think?"

Tears glistened in her eyes. She didn't say a word as one trickled down her cheek.

He would say the words. "I need you. He needs you. Say you'll stay."

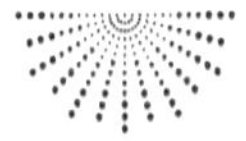

The bed creaked slightly. Was Hawke getting up? She wasn't going to let her warmth source go. Not just yet. She snuggled in further under the blankets, nuzzling backward while her nude body sought out the furnace that Hawke created with his muscular body.

A hand—Hawke's, of course, who else's?—ran over her thigh, leaving goose bumps where it had gently coursed. His hand crept lower, over the curve of her ass, lingering, tracing tiny circles with the pad of his thumb, circles growing larger and larger.

She repressed the urge to moan, not wanting to break the beauty of the silence. Outside, she could see in the dawn's light the falling of snow glistening in the rays. She relaxed, leaning backward. So easy to sleep next to this man who'd given her his heart, soul, and his bear. Easy to sleep except for one thing. There between her legs, his touch had awakened a passion for him that was relentless, throbbing and pulsing, screaming for his touch.

Damn.

And then the moan, well, that telltale moan, it escaped her in the form of a low groan melded with a sigh.

That seemed to be the equivalent of pushing a start button for Hawke. Seconds later his warm breath was near the nape of her neck. A shiver ran over her, one that had nothing to do with the chill outside.

His tongue touched that sensitive spot behind her earlobe. His arm had wrapped itself around her torso, pulling her close. His hardness was there, prevalent, obvious, and so very delectable. His hips shifted, grinding that length against her body. She arched backward, pressing her ass against his hard-on, moved her body just so.

"You know what that does to me, woman."

Oh, yeah, she knew. She'd known since their first time, almost a month ago when he'd come in after building cabins for the other shifters—all of them opted to stay on his property to become a clan. He'd been working, smelling deliciously male and musky as he darted for the shower. She thought of that first time, the shower's steam, his erection.

She moaned, just thinking about it and wiggled her body more, driving his hardness against her tush.

She heard a rumble that signified one thing, and

one thing alone: his bear's presence. She turned to face him, looking deeply into his eyes, seeing his bear, seeing the love that both of them had for her. The lengths they'd go to in order to protect what was theirs.

He lowered his head, taking one dusky nipple into his mouth, sucking fiercely while his other hand cupped her breast, his fingers squeezing her nipple, throwing her into a chasm of ecstasy she'd have a hard time climbing out of.

"Hawke." His name ripped from her throat with passion as he paid particular tribute to her breasts with his hands and mouth. "God, Hawke. Don't make me wait."

He loved teasing her, building her to a crescendo, then taking her over the edge with his lovemaking. She mewled, digging her fingers into his shoulders, her nails marking flesh, seeking purchase as she tried to pull him into position.

He lay firm, relentless in his pursuit of her nipple, circling the tip with his tongue, teasing, then releasing it, his tongue tracing a slick trail over her creamy breast, blowing cool air in his tongue's wake. She lowered her hand from his shoulder, reaching for his erection when he grasped her wrist in a powerful hold and brought it above her head. He trapped the other wrist, holding both captive.

"Damn you," she hissed, enjoying his roughness merged with the sweet torture of his foreplay.

He ground his hips against her, that hardness

pressing on her mound, making her clit buzz with need. "You'll pay," she threatened.

"I'll pay every day for the rest of my life," he said against her navel. "And I want nothing more than to pay. Just like this."

And with that, he lowered his head. Her legs parted as if they had a mind of their own. With his free hand, he spread her lips, and blew that cool breath that threw her over the edge again.

"What was that you said about paying?" With every word, every breath, the air he blew teased her.

Her body arched upward, wanting him. He flicked his tongue out, tracing a circle around the sensitive bud on fire for him.

"Please, Hawke." Yes, she'd resort to pleading if that would get her what—

"Oh, God, yes." She gasped the words.

His mouth was fully enclosed around her clit, sucking, releasing, flicking, licking. A pattern of movements that had no pattern at all, they were pushing her too close to a place she wanted to share with his body. His thumb alit on her sensitive button at the same moment he thrust his tongue inside her.

Alannah flinched and jerked her hands free, grabbing his head, pushing it in, her nails digging into flesh, her thighs clamped around his head.

Tiny lights flickered behind her closed lids as she whimpered her pleasure. One final plunge of his tongue and she grabbed his hair tightly, fisting it, pushing his head down at the same time, thrusting her hips up.

"Hawke." His name was one long extended release from her lips as her body yielded to the pleasure he delivered.

And before she could finish, he'd positioned himself and thrust his hardness deeply inside her pulsing muscles.

"Fuck. That feels good."

"Mhm mmmm." She agreed whole heartedly as he began to pump into her, driving deeply, over and over. His chest scraped against her nipples when he put his arm beneath her and pulled her close to a sitting position, letting her ride him while he pushed her up and then drove her down, impaling her body, branding her inside.

"Hawke?" She gasped, grabbing his shoulders. "Wait."

"Hmmm?" He pulled back and looked in her eyes, his own sex-glazed and heavy-lidded.

"I want you to couplebond me. I want you to make me yours." She panted, breathless.

"You know about that?" His words came out in faltered pauses while he tried to even his breathing.

"Fiona told me when we talked yesterday."

"You sure?"

"More than anything. More than ever."

"You're so fucking sexy right now. Sexier than you've ever been." His eyes flashed a silver glow. He thrust into her, picking up the momentum with a ferociousness that was taking her to another dimension. She grabbed his shoulders, riding him, watching his beautiful face as lust and love merged, melded, and chased each other across his countenance.

"Fuck, Alannah." With that, he roared, the sound seeming to come from deep within his soul, then bared his teeth and lowered his head.

The sting was fierce, but easily abated by the licking that Fiona had told her would lessen the pain. She felt his thickness as he came undone within her while she rolled into wave after wave of orgasms. She had aftershock following aftershock while he held her.

When she'd finally stopped, he held her gently as if she'd break, her head against his chest, their bodies merged as one.

Round two was no less spectacular than the first time around until finally she laid her head on his shoulder and slept.

Hours later, Alannah and Hawke padded out to the kitchen. Mireille and Renee were up already, having breakfast.

"About time, sleepyheads." Mireille giggled.

"What are you two plotting?" Alanna mockingly waggled her finger at them.

"Who us?" Renee grinned. "Mireille was telling me she wanted to find out about an apprenticeship."

"Isn't that what brought you here to Russia?" Hawke laughed. "Isn't that what got you abducted? Seeking an apprenticeship?"

Mireille nodded solemnly. "Yes, I was going to study to be a healer."

"You're not anymore?"

"No." Mireille glanced at Renee.

"So what do you want to study then?" Alannah asked, wondering what that glance was about.

"Transformation and reversal spells."

"Is this because of Jenner?" Hawke teased.

Mireille fake-gasped. "No, of course not." But her cheeks were a traitorous shade of pink, belying her words. "I wouldn't mind seeing Jenner again. I called Mikhail. He said he'd ask Desideria to see if they would take apprentices."

Alannah shook her head at her little sister, who suddenly didn't seem so little anymore. "I doubt they'd take an apprentice. They're part of the Circle."

The Circle, an elite group of witches and wizards. Not likely to find themselves interested in training a witch who'd barely mastered intermediate spell casting. But Alannah didn't want to discourage her sister. She gave her a smile and a hug. "I hope they give you a chance."

"And you'd leave me here? Alone?" Renee's voice was playfully panicky.

"Alone?" Mireille shrieked. "Hawke's got shifters galore here. Lots of them."

"But you're my best friend."

"Maybe they'll let me bring someone along."

This time Alannah didn't contain her laughter.

Pipe dreams.

Under the table, Hawke took her hand in his, tugging her closer. She leaned into him, kissing his cheek, relishing the scent of him.

"It's snowing," he whispered. "Cuddling weather."

"And to think, I didn't used to like Russia."

"No?" He quirked a brow teasingly.

"Now, I think I could live here for a while."

"Perhaps forever?" He put a thumb under her chin, tipping her head his way.

"Forever after," she countered, raising her lips to his, tasting the scent of the man who'd be her forever man.

Forever after.

KEEP READING FOR AN EXCERPT FROM THE NEXT Shifters Forever Worlds book!

Circe Brazos is notorious. Notoriously hard. Notoriously bad ass. Notoriously alone. And she's damned happy that way. Don't give her any complications in her black and white world.

Circe's a shifter elemental hybrid. One of the very few who exist. Too often these hybrids do not make it to adulthood. The fact that she and her siblings did has made them uniquely qualified to run the Order of Elementals—a secret group designed to assist elementals, particularly those who share a host with a shifter.

Long ago, Circe kicked Mae Forrester out of her life. Now Mae's back, and Circe has to deal with the reasons Mae left. As if that's not bad enough, a gorgeous hunk of a shifter shows up on her doorstep with a little girl hybrid who desperately needs Circe's help. Except, Circe didn't know at the end of the day who needed help more—herself or the young hybrid.

Lincoln Avila has a damned good reason for hating elementals. They've torn everything in his life apart. Now he has to deal with the fact that his niece, his ward, is a hybrid. Thought that was bad, did you, Linc? Here's bad, for real. Don't fall in love with Circe, the hybrid elemental bad ass who has no fondness for gray areas or men. The beautiful, notorious, curvy hybrid has found a way to wrap herself around his heart. Convincing her to let love win won't necessarily be easy.

That's okay, Linc's up for a challenge. He just has no idea the challenge could lead to life or death—his own.

CHAPTER 1

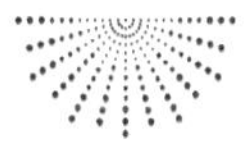

"Mae's coming." Circe Brazos scowled at her brother and sisters.

Marco her brother, the only brother she had—not to mention, her best friend, at least these days—lounged in the chair by the pool, stretched out, his lean muscular body absorbing the sun's rays. Her sisters, *the twins*, as everyone called them, Camden and Eden were lying on their stomachs on towels, reading, letting the sun caress their voluptuous curves.

Hell, Circe was no stranger to curves, or voluptuousness. She had that market cornered with way more curves than she'd ever wanted when she was a teen. These days though, she appreciated her curves, relishing every inch of her body. She rolled over, pushed her sunglasses down so she could let Marco see her eyes—see the anger within. Deep within her, her elemental, Albani sizzled with fury. Albani was an electric elemental, and even more easily angered than Circe.

Marco raised his brow and put his phone down, mid-text. "You make it sound like the world's coming to an end."

Circe sat up with a huff. "You don't think there's a problem? After all the—"

Near the pool, a lightbulb shattered. Then another. Circe breathed deeply to gain control of Albani's anger, her own anger, before they had to spend a fortune replacing the bulbs Albani was destroying.

The twins put their magazines down and looked at her, a question in their eyes.

They didn't know her full history with Mae. She'd never shared. The only one she'd shared this with was Marco, a panther shifter elemental hybrid, just like her.

All four of the Brazos siblings were shifter elemental hybrids. Rare in the world. Even rarer, to have them be in the same family. It was no surprise the Order of Elementals had put the Brazos siblings in charge of the Order's business, a business that was highly secretive, but crucial to shifters who found themselves with an elemental residing within.

Elementals had been known to kill their shifter hosts, and then they would move on, finding another host, just as they did with humans. But with the longevity and power of shifters, it made the relationship tenuous at best. Unless the shifter and the elemental could find a middle ground. No easy task.

That's where the Brazos siblings and the Order of Elementals came in.

Circe, Marco, Camden, and Eden were specialists at this. So, they were the powerhouse of the Order, and led by Circe as the first born.

"She wants something, you know." Circe was still on the same topic.

The topic of Mae.

Mae.

Circe fought back a sneer.

"Yes, she does," Marco answered.

Fury surged within Circe. Her skin burned with static electricity, making tiny crackling sounds she couldn't control. Betrayal seethed within her, disappointment in her brother.

"You talked to her." She let the words come from between her lips in a staccato. "You. Talked. To. Her." She sucked air in and closed her eyes against the anger.

"I answered the call." Marco's voice was clipped. "We are the Order. We have a duty. A sworn duty," he reminded her.

Circe opened tortured eyes, her dark gaze tormented by the past. "Yes." She nodded, then whispered, "We do."

What's next?

Notorious

Another book of the Shifters Forever Worlds, a place teeming with shifters!

~

Please refer to the website for newest releases as we spend time with our Shifters Forever and all the wonderful spin off series!

ElleThorne.com

Thank you for reading!

SHIFTERS FOREVER SERIES

Are you ready for it?
I have a whole world full of shifters to share with you.
I'm listing them here, in the suggested reading order,
though I've tried to make it so that you can pick up
anywhere in the series as we all have probably done
that at one point or another.
Many of these are organized in box sets for savings. Be
sure to visit www.ellethorne.com to see which box sets
are out!

Where's the best place to start? Well, probably with
SHIFTERS FOREVER.

SHIFTERS FOREVER

Grizzly bear shifters and their mates steam up the pages in these swoon-worthy paranormal romances. From trespassers with hidden agendas to curvaceous women who are ready to take a chance, the stories in this collection will capture your heart.

- PROTECTION
- SEDUCTION
- PERSUASION
- INVITATION
- TEMPTATION
- ATTRACTION

~

ALWAYS AFTER DARK

A spinoff with the white tiger from Shifters Forever: Vax, born Vittorio Tiero. He's the one that helped Kane out during a shifter battle. Follow the Tiero family, a group of white tiger shifters, as they head to America to find love... and heart-stopping danger. Full of romance, suspense, and gritty drama, this red-hot collection is sure to entertain!

- CONTROVERSY
- TERRITORY
- ADVERSARY
- SANCTUARY

~

NEVER AFTER DARK

Another spinoff that takes place in Europe. Here we visit cities along the Mediterranean and meet the old school Tiero white tiger shifters who are resistant to change.

- FORBIDDEN
- FORSAKEN
- FORGOTTEN
- FOREPLAY

ONLY AFTER DARK

Taking place in New Orleans, the Arceneaux shifters, led by Lézare, Vax's white tiger cousin—on his mother's side—are sure to capture your hearts. The Arceneaux are the black sheep of the family. Lézare doesn't cave to public opinion. He dictates policy in the area he rules and he shuns old school European rules and regimes.

- DESIRABLE
- INSATIABLE
- COMBUSTIBLE
- UNDENIABLE
- INEVITABLE
- INESCAPABLE

BITTER FALLS FOREVER

This romance features Mae Forester's nephew Dane Forester, a freewheeling, sexy, successful, movie star who uses every role and every woman to escape and forget the heartbreak he left in Bitter Falls.

- UNBOUND

BARELY AFTER DARK

This series features more of Mae Forester's nephews! Grizzly bear shifters steam up the pages in these swoon-worthy paranormal romances. From trespassers with hidden agendas to curvaceous women who are ready to take a chance, the stories in this collection will capture your heart.

- CROSS
- LANCE
- JUDGE

EVER AFTER DARK

Get ready to be introduced to the white tigers you learned to love in Always After Dark, Never After Dark, and Only After Dark. See their heritage. Visit Giovanni Tiero and his brothers Federico and Tito. Get reacquainted with Isabel Tiero and meet her sister Capriana Valenti.

- STONEBOUND
- FORMIDABLE

SHIFTERS FOREVER AFTER

This series follows a group of polar bears in New York. Russian and rumored to be mobbed up, they are a powerhouse of shifters, determining the fate of many on the East Coast. Mikhail Romanoff, Layla's father, runs this outfit with an iron fist. Layla's sexy cousin Malachi features prominently in this series.

- COMPLICATION
- FASCINATION
- MOTIVATION
- CAPTIVATION
- FLIRTATION
- INFATUATION

FOREVER AFTER DARK

A series which takes place in Denver, Colorado. Enter a world of secrets and forbidden love. Panther shifters who who share their worlds with elementals must decide who they can trust—and who they can't live without.

- NOTORIOUS
- SCANDALOUS

- DELICIOUS
- PERILOUS

SHIFTERS FOREVER MORE Grizzly bear shifters, dragon shifters, sorceresses, elementals, and all types of other paranormal beings and their mates steam up the pages as the Bear Canyon Valley clan sorts through trespassers with hidden agenda, hidden military compounds, top secret experiments and curvaceous women who are ready to take a chance. The romances in this collection will capture your heart and leave your head spinning!

- CONFUSION
- DECISION
- POSSESSION
- ILLUSION
- PASSION
- IMPRESSION

FINALLY AFTER DARK
Follow a pack of dire wolves as they encounter Valkyrie and Berserkers and determine the origins of their kind throughout the ages, while discovering their fated mates.

- ORIGINS
- CHALLENGE
- DAMAGE
- RAVAGE
- MORE TO FOLLOW!

I do hope you'll be able to join me on this wonderful journey with our Shifters Forever Worlds Shifters and their mates!

To receive exclusive updates from Elle Thorne and to be the first to get your hands on the next release, please sign up for her mailing list.

Elle Thorne Newsletter

If you can't click, just put this in your browser: http://www.ellethorne.com/contact

MY PERSONAL GUARANTEE:
THIS WILL ONLY BE USED TO ANNOUNCE NEW RELEASES AND SPECIALS. AND TO GIVE MY WONDERFUL SPECIAL READERS A LITTLE GIFT.

SHIFTERS REALMS

I have another new world of shifters! How exciting! I can't wait to share them with you!

Be sure to visit www.ellethorne.com to see which ones are out!

Where's the best place to start? Here we go!

IRON FLATS

Wolf shifters and their mates steam up the pages in these paranormal romances. From rovers with hidden agendas to women who are ready to take a chance, to unknown the stories in this collection will capture your heart.

- Iron Flats Exile
- Iron Flats Justice
- Iron Flats Rebel
- Iron Flats Maverick

More to follow!

I do hope you'll be able to join me on this wonderful journey with our Shifters Forever Worlds Shifters and their mates!

To receive exclusive updates from Elle Thorne and to be the first to get your hands on the next release, please sign up for her mailing list.

Elle Thorne Newsletter

If you can't click, just put this in your browser: http://www.ellethorne.com/contact

My personal guarantee:

This will only be used to announce new releases and specials. And to give my wonderful special readers a little gift.

Shifters Forever Worlds

Shifter Realms

For sales and news, sign up for the newsletter! Thank you for purchasing and downloading my book. Words can't express what it means to me. If you enjoyed this read, please remember to take a second to leave a review. I'd love to know what your favorite parts were.

The fun isn't about to stop. Make sure you sign up for the link to the newsletter.

Hearing from you means the world to me. This would not be possible without you and your love for reading.

With much gratitude, I thank you!

It took Elle Thorne years to stop being a closet romantic.

Originally from Europe, she wouldn't dream of living anywhere else but Texas. Unless it was another southern—translation: warm!—state. A southern European by birth, she wants to be near the water and the Mediterranean temperatures if possible.

Where does she like to hang out? Near a lake, a beach, preferably with a latte—extra shot of espresso, please! She's inspired by the everyday men who make dreams come true. She loves a roughneck, especially one with a callous or two on his hands. A man who knows how to fix a car, please a woman, and protect what's his.

Nothing less will do.

To receive exclusive updates from Elle Thorne and to be the first to get your hands on the next release, please sign up for her mailing list.
Put this in your browser:
www.ellethorne.com/contact

My personal guarantee:
This will only be used to announce new releases and specials. And to give my wonderful special readers a little gift.

www.ingramcontent.com/pod-product-compliance
Lightning Source LLC
Chambersburg PA
CBHW031131130726
47988CB00006B/2320